Only Tanner's quick reaction kept Addie from falling all the way in when he grabbed her with both hands.

Both big hands that pulled her up and set her back on her feet.

And then stayed around her waist.

Great big hands that she could feel the strength of.

Great big hands that for some odd reason caused goose bumps to erupt on the surface of her arms.

And made her miss them when he finally took them away...

"Okay, it's probably better if we don't talk about any of this stuff so I can concentrate on what I'm doing," she said, looking up at that handsome face just above her.

Tanner nodded again, ~~his~~ ext~~remely~~ blue eyes peering ~~to~~ ~~be~~ unders~~

And sor~~ ~~cipher.

It wasn't ~~

In fact, it w~~ ...a man-woman thing...

* * *

THE CAMDENS OF MONTANA: Four military brothers falling in love in Big Sky Country!

Dear Reader,

We're back in Merritt, Montana, where Addie Markham has had a rough year and a half. She's lost her mother, father and sister, become the guardian to her newborn niece, Poppy, and now she's been left at the altar. When marine Tanner Camden shows up claiming he may be Poppy's father, it's the last blow.

Tough marine Tanner has discovered the one thing that terrifies him—the possibility that he's a father. But, determined to do the right thing if he is, he makes a deal with Addie to trade his handyman skills for caregiving lessons. In the process, the two—who begin at odds—find common ground that leads to an overwhelming attraction to each other.

But if Tanner proves to be Poppy's dad, that means he'll take away the only family Addie has now—the baby she loves.

Is Tanner tough enough to do that to her? Or are his feelings for her stronger? We'll see...

Happy reading,

Victoria Pade

The Marine's Baby Blues

VICTORIA PADE

HARLEQUIN
SPECIAL
EDITION

If you purchased this book without a cover you should be aware
that this book is stolen property. It was reported as "unsold and
destroyed" to the publisher, and neither the author nor the
publisher has received any payment for this "stripped book."

HARLEQUIN®
SPECIAL
EDITION™

Recycling programs
for this product may
not exist in your area.

ISBN-13: 978-1-335-40486-2

The Marine's Baby Blues

Copyright © 2021 by Victoria Pade

All rights reserved. No part of this book may be used or reproduced in
any manner whatsoever without written permission except in the case of
brief quotations embodied in critical articles and reviews.

This is a work of fiction. Names, characters, places and incidents
are either the product of the author's imagination or are used fictitiously.
Any resemblance to actual persons, living or dead, businesses,
companies, events or locales is entirely coincidental.

This edition published by arrangement with Harlequin Books S.A.

For questions and comments about the quality of this book,
please contact us at CustomerService@Harlequin.com.

Harlequin Enterprises ULC
22 Adelaide St. West, 40th Floor
Toronto, Ontario M5H 4E3, Canada
www.Harlequin.com

Printed in U.S.A.

Victoria Pade is a *USA TODAY* bestselling author of numerous romance novels. She has two beautiful and talented daughters—Cori and Erin—and is a native of Colorado, where she lives and writes. A devoted chocolate lover, she's in search of the perfect chocolate-chip-cookie recipe.

For information about her latest and upcoming releases, visit Victoria Pade on Facebook—she would love to hear from you.

Books by Victoria Pade

Harlequin Special Edition

The Camdens of Montana

The Marine Makes Amends

Camden Family Secrets

The Marine Makes His Match
AWOL Bride
Special Forces Father
The Marine's Family Mission

The Camdens of Colorado

A Camden's Baby Secret
Abby, Get Your Groom
A Sweetheart for the Single Dad
Her Baby and Her Beau
To Catch a Camden
A Camden Family Wedding

Montana Mavericks: Rust Creek Cowboys

The Maverick's Christmas Baby

Montana Mavericks: Striking It Rich

A Family for the Holidays

Visit the Author Profile page
at Harlequin.com for more titles.

Chapter One

"Please, please, *please* stop apologizing, Gloria. It was *not* your fault!" Addie Markham said to her late mother's best friend, one *please* added for each of Gloria's so-sorrys today alone.

"But it was me who recommended Stephanie—"

"Because at the time you were doing a good deed for her and for me. And I appreciated it, and that does not make you responsible for the way things turned out. What's done is done. Let's put it behind us," Addie begged of the woman she'd always liked and thought highly of.

Putting this latest bombshell behind her was something Addie was eager to do.

It had been six days since she'd been left at the altar. The original plan had been for Addie and fiancé Sean Barkley to have a Sunday afternoon ceremony and reception in the lovely backyard garden that Gloria had offered as the wedding site.

From there they were to spend their wedding night at the bed-and-breakfast in their small Montana hometown of Merritt. Monday and Tuesday they planned to return wedding paraphernalia and clean up Gloria's yard so it would be in the same shape they'd found it, and leave on Wednesday for their honeymoon.

Best-laid plans. Instead, here Addie was on the following Saturday afternoon, unmarried and on her own.

Sean had taken off on "their" honeymoon without her. And since Addie felt strongly that it wasn't fair to make Gloria suffer any more inconveniences, all post-wedding duties had landed on Addie alone. Along with the task of packing up her infant niece Poppy's things and hers to move out of Sean's apartment and into her late grandmother's house before Sean returned tomorrow.

With Addie's closest friend, Kelly, signed on to babysit Poppy until Addie could get her head above water, she'd spent the first post-wedding day returning rental chairs and tables that she would otherwise have been charged a late fee for, and dealing with all the uneaten reception food.

But after that she'd needed to accept Gloria's patience so she could switch her attention to her grandmother's old house that was sorely in need of a complete overhaul.

Since Tuesday Addie had been working at clearing cobwebs and cleaning. She'd gotten one of the house's two bathrooms in operating order, either repaired or replaced kitchen appliances and the water heater, and begun to deal with the lead paint that needed to be encapsulated in order to make the house safe for the two-and-a-half month old she was now guardian of.

So far she hadn't been able to repaint more than the room she'd designated as the nursery, and wanting to make the nursery less dismal than the rest of the house, she'd also put a little time into decorating it.

Now Addie was concentrating on the wedding gifts. They would all have to be returned, but until she found the time for that, she was transferring them from Gloria's place to the house.

Gloria's arthritis had forced her to agree not to do any of the post-wedding work herself and she was being very understanding of Addie's inability to do everything immediately, but Addie knew it was an imposition to have the presents piled in the older woman's living room. It was bad enough that she hadn't yet been able to put the yard completely back in order; she wanted her mother's friend to at least have things out of the way inside.

What Gloria *was* insisting on helping with today, though, was to load Addie's small sedan, stringing one apology after another along the way and prompting Addie to beg her to stop.

They returned to the house where Addie picked

up as many gift boxes as she could carry and Gloria took a large unwrapped silver tray as they retraced their steps outside.

"This is just a minor setback for you," the older woman said along the way. "You'll find someone even better than Sean, just wait and see."

Oh no, on to the pity part, Addie thought, hating that. Sympathy was one thing—there had been a lot of that during the last year, first over the death of her dad, then her mom, then Della. For the most part that had been comforting, supportive, helpful.

But pity was something else altogether. It made her seem pathetically weak and helpless. And she wasn't weak or helpless, and she certainly didn't want to be considered pathetic.

So she didn't say anything in response to Gloria's assurance, merely continuing to load the boxes into her back seat.

Once she had, she turned to take the tray from Gloria. But rather than handing it over and stepping back, Gloria held it up like a mirror and said, "Just look at you—new men will be clamoring after you."

Cornered in the L of the car's open door by the older woman, Addie couldn't escape her own reflection.

And the image that stared back at her was evidence enough that Gloria was just being kind. Addie could see for herself that she looked the worse for wear.

She'd been too swamped to put any effort into her auburn hair since the wedding that wasn't. Beyond shampooing it and brushing out the below-her-shoulders mass, she'd merely caught it all straight back into a serviceable ponytail.

There was almost no color in her face and since she'd eaten very little this week, her cheeks had taken a slight dip.

The brown eyes that had been voted Best Eyes by her high school senior class seemed unspectacular to her without liner or mascara, and while her lips were a natural mauve, she judged them blah now, too. Especially adorned with nothing but colorless lip balm.

Adding to it the fact that she'd always wished she was taller than her five-foot-three-inch height, and did not have what anyone would consider a voluptuous chest, she was all the more convinced that Gloria was merely trying to boost her morale with exaggeration. Her mother's friend was still at it. "You've grown up to be the prettiest of all the Markhams. If I'd looked like you do at your age… the fun I would have had… A natural beauty, that's what you are. And other men will take notice. Just be prepared!"

"I don't really want them to," Addie said honestly. "I was with Sean before Poppy came along, but now that he's out of the picture I need to focus on her, on being her mom, on the little family she and I are now. The only family I have. It's going to be a long time before I let anyone else into that—for her sake and for mine."

Addie was wearing an old pair of torn jeans and a

white tank top that she'd covered with a striped shirt until the heat of the June day and all the moving had made her too hot. Now the shirt was tied around her waist and, as if to give her statement more oomph, she pulled on the ends of the knot to tighten it.

"I know that's how you feel because you've been so horribly hurt," Gloria said with more of that commiseration Addie hated so much. "But you'll change your mind. I promise you will. When the right man comes along—"

Right or wrong, a man did come along just as those words left Gloria's mouth.

Or at least a man in a big white pickup truck pulled into the curb behind Addie's car and directly in front of Gloria's house.

The attention of both women was drawn in that direction by his arrival.

"Someone to see you?" Addie asked Gloria because she didn't immediately recognize the man behind the wheel. But he'd pulled up so close to her rear bumper that he seemed to be joining them, and anything or anyone who could put an end to this conversation was welcome as far as she was concerned.

"I don't know who that is…" Gloria said, sounding as clueless as Addie was.

The truck door opened then and out climbed the driver.

Who was one heck of a man…

He was well over six feet tall—probably four inches over—and dressed in military boots, camo pants and a tan crewneck T-shirt that also looked military-issue but fitted him like a second skin.

It crossed Addie's mind that maybe T-shirts weren't made large enough to be any looser on him, because his shoulders were a mile wide, his chest was as broad and muscular as they came, and his biceps were enormous works of art.

His remarkable torso did shrink down to a narrow waist and hips, only to show more muscles in thick thighs.

"Hubba-hubba," she heard Gloria whisper, making Addie realize that she'd taken in the body before the face. She adjusted her view upward.

Only to agree with the older woman's dated assessment.

Because the man's face was enough to make her eyes widen.

Precision-cut short dark-brown-almost-black hair framed a square-ish forehead with full eyebrows arched over eyes that were a unique blue.

A piercing, penetrating cobalt blue that gave Addie her first inkling of who the man was, because the only eyes she'd ever seen like that belonged to the Camdens.

But which Camden was he?

Not the oldest, Micah, who had returned to Merritt several months ago to start a small batch brewery. Addie had run into him in town numerous times. So this had to be one of the triplets.

One of the triplets who—like his older brother only better—had grown into a staggeringly handsome man with a somewhat narrow, very straight nose; a not-too-full, not-too-thin mouth that gave nothing of his emotions away; and an all-round bone structure that chiseled his cheekbones and his cleanly-shaven jawline into starkly masculine and undeniably gorgeous angles.

"Are you Addie Markham?" he asked, his focus steadfastly on her, his voice as deep and commanding as his body was impressive.

What now? was her first thought because so much had been thrown at her in the last year that she'd begun to instinctively expect the worst.

But denying who she was wouldn't help, so she said, "I am."

And then logical reasoning kicked in. If this guy was one of the Camden triplets stopping to talk to her, it was likely Della's old high school sweetheart looking to give condolences.

She relaxed.

"Tanner Camden?" she guessed as he strode purposefully from the side of his truck toward Addie and Gloria—who had stepped far enough away to free Addie from being cornered and was also facing their new arrival.

He nodded just once to confirm his identity.

"Oh, that's right, I heard you were home for a visit," Gloria said then.

In all the turmoil of her wedding that wasn't, Addie hadn't heard that.

Gloria's comment drew his glance to the other

woman, though. "Miss Gloria," he greeted. "How've you been?"

Gloria giggled like a girl and skipped the list of health problems she usually told everyone about, to say in a vaguely coquettish voice, "I'm just dandy."

"Happy to hear that," he said politely before putting on just a little charm to say, "Could I ask a favor of you? Do you think I might talk to Addie alone?"

"Oh, of course!" the older woman said, partly as if she was eager to please him, and partly with more of the compassionate tone that made Addie think Gloria had come to the same conclusion— that Tanner was there to express his sympathies for Della's death.

Then, to Addie, she said, "I'll just be inside, honey."

Addie nodded and slid her gaze back onto Tanner, whom she hadn't seen since she was eleven—when he'd still just been a reedy seventeen-going-on-eighteen-year-old whose skin hadn't yet cleared and who hadn't been any sort of preview at all of the man he'd turned into.

Despite Addie's attention being on him again, he continued to watch Gloria until she reached her front door and went inside. Which seemed odd to Addie, because in all of the condolences for her father, her mother *and* Della, no one had needed privacy to convey them.

But only when he knew the older woman was well out of earshot did he refocus on Addie.

"You've been two steps ahead of me for a couple of days."

"I have?" she said, surprised that he might have been so actively looking for her. She'd been thinking that he must have just driven by Gloria's house on his way to somewhere else, spotted her and decided to stop.

"I've needed to talk to you, but for some reason no one is too sure where you're living. I was told you'd *been* living with some guy, that I could check there, but every time I went to the apartment there was no answer. Then someone said you might be in an old house that I think used to belong to your grandmother. But that place doesn't look livable, so I wasn't surprised when you weren't there—"

"It's been a busy week," Addie said without explanation.

"Somebody finally told me you might be staying with a friend, so I went there today, and she told me you'd either be at the apartment I've been going to or the old house or here. So I went back to the other two places, and *finally*, here you are."

Apparently he hadn't wanted to contact her by phone?

And had he been so diligently searching for her just to give condolences? Or was there more to it?

Maybe he was looking for some memento of Della to remember her by?

But with the way things between them had ended, Addie thought that seemed a little far-fetched. Unless he wanted something of his that Della had kept, something that Addie hadn't realized was his when she'd gone through the stuff her sister had left behind. Which might be a problem if Addie had thrown it away...

"Well, you've found me," she said, hoping he would get to whatever he was after so she could finish all she still needed to do.

"I understand Della...passed away," he said more solemnly then, searching for the least disturbing euphemism like so many had before him.

"Two and a half months ago," Addie answered quietly. Even anticipating this didn't make it easy for her to talk about her late sister.

"I'm sorry," he said. "I couldn't believe it when I heard."

"It was unexpected...a shock all the way around..." Because while Della might have been almost six and a half years older than Addie's twenty-seven, she'd still been young and healthy and at no risk in having Poppy. Until her blood pressure had spiked during delivery and a previously undiagnosed aneurysm in her heart had taken her life.

"How did it happen?" Tanner Camden asked.

Addie told him.

"So it's true...she did have a baby," he said then, as if he'd been hoping it had only been a rumor.

"A little girl. Poppy," Addie said, wondering why that seemed to be of note to him.

But he left her hanging while he closed his eyes as if he needed time for that information to sink in, slowly nodding his head as he did.

Then he stopped nodding, raised his well-sculpted chin and opened those beautiful blue eyes as he took a breath and exhaled with something that sounded like resignation.

"I also heard that Della wouldn't say who the father was, so she died without anyone knowing... Any chance she told you?"

"No. She said after the baby was born she would, but..." Addie's voice cracked and she cleared her throat of the emotions the memory caused. "She died before that could happen."

"And no one has come forward?"

"I have," she said firmly, wondering if he was considering some grand gesture like volunteering to take the unclaimed baby of his old girlfriend.

"Yeah, I also heard that you'd taken the baby on. But you haven't found so much as a clue who fathered it?"

"Her," Addie corrected with a bit of a bite in her tone. "No, I don't know who fathered *her*," she finished, the schoolteacher in her showing.

Tanner Camden's broad shoulders straightened and became somehow wider, as if he was reporting for duty.

Then, just when Addie thought the grand gesture was coming, he said in a quiet, grave tone, "I think the baby might be mine."

"Yours? Poppy can't be yours!" Addie blurted out, thinking that a grand gesture made more sense than his assertion.

Clearly uncomfortable, he said, "Eleven and a half months ago I was in town on leave—"

"I know." Although she hadn't seen him and couldn't recall the exact date, she *had* heard that he'd come to visit his grandfather. She'd heard about it from Della, who had not made any big deal of it. To Addie's surprise and relief.

"Della and I spent the night together," he confessed under his breath, as if he wasn't proud of it.

"You did not!" Addie shot back. "You had coffee with her one afternoon—she told me. She said she'd wanted to tell you how sorry she was for all that drama when the two of you graduated high school. She told me that you accepted her apology, went your separate ways, and that was that. She said she didn't see you the whole rest of the time you were here."

"She didn't," he said. "But my grandfather was giving me a ride to Billings to catch a plane at the end of my leave and it worked out better for him if I went the night before my flight and stayed in a hotel. I ran into Della again there, at the hotel. She said she was treating herself to a little time in the city before meeting a friend from college who was coming in the next day—"

"Della didn't go to college," Addie countered as if she was catching him in multiple lies.

But underneath it, her own fears were mounting.

Tanner Camden frowned in what appeared to be some confusion of his own now. "She told me over coffee that she went to UCLA. That she got a degree in business, came back here and went to work for the bank your dad used to manage. She told me she was about to be promoted to manager herself."

"There was no college, no degree. Della never left Merritt. Dad got her the job at the bank. She started as a teller and she was still a teller..." Addie stalled, fearing the worst.

Working not to show any of her own trepidations, she went on. "So there was no *friend from college* for her to be meeting," she concluded, once more as if nothing he claimed could be true and have led him to be Poppy's father.

But Tanner wasn't getting defensive, he just seemed to be perplexed. "She lied... Was it just an excuse to follow me to Billings?"

"I never heard anything about her *going* to Billings. She said she saw you for coffee and that was it," Addie insisted, sounding defensive herself.

"Look, I'm not making this up. We ran into each other at the hotel," Tanner continued matter-of-factly. "Over coffee in town she'd seemed to have her act together... I mean, I had the impression that she'd grown up, that our past was behind us. So when I saw her again and she suggested we have dinner, I said okay. Then we went clubbing. There was a lot of drinking. We ended up spending the night together," he finished in a voice that was barely audible, again as if wasn't proud of it.

Addie's stomach was beginning to knot and she was very much afraid that denying what he was telling her wasn't going to make it go away. Or him, either. And if it was possible that he was Poppy's father, then suddenly she was looking at the potential of losing the baby she considered hers...

"Two months ago I was in Washington, DC," he was saying. "And I ran into Scooter Thompson—he was in my class—"

"He's our dentist now. He doesn't like that nickname any more. He wants to be called Harvey." As if that mattered...

Tanner ignored her footnote.

"He was visiting in-laws. Anyway, he asked me if I knew about Della, told me she'd died having a baby. A baby whose father Della had kept a secret..."

And you weren't fishing for the information to see if you should step in and be a hero, Addie thought. *You were hoping I knew, so you'd be off the hook...*

She wanted to kick herself for not having realized that before. For not using whatever opportunity there might have been for her to lie and tell him she *did* know who the father was and it *wasn't* him.

But she'd been honest...

It was her own fear that spurred her to say, "Poppy is mine! I was in the delivery room. It was my arms they put her in the minute she was born, while they worked on Della. I was at the hospital with her for the whole three days she needed to be there after the difficult birth. It's my arms she's been in ever since!"

"Is she okay?" he asked.

"She's fine. She's great. She's mine!" Addie repeated, feeling as if she might break down and fighting not to.

Whether or not Tanner Camden realized what was going on with her, his voice took on a softness as he said, "But if I'm her father I have to know."

Addie had lost too much in the last year; she wasn't going to lose Poppy. "She's my family. All that's left of it!" she said in near panic.

"I have to know," he repeated just as gently, but more firmly. "If you don't know that someone else is her father then I think we have to have my DNA and the baby's DNA compared."

Was it too late to lie, to make up a story, to say she did know?

Addie desperately wanted to believe it wasn't, but she knew better.

So instead, scornfully, she said, "Didn't you use protection?"

Once more clearly uncomfortable, he said, "Let's just say that Della took the lead with that…" He stalled, sighed, and then reluctantly and with embarrassment and a hint of anger, said, "If there was a…*problem* that could have caused this…she didn't tell me."

But Addie had no doubt that if there was a way to sabotage things and give herself even the smallest chance of trapping Tanner with a real pregnancy, Della would have taken it. Even all these years later.

Or maybe more so all these years later, after her sister's succession of failed relationships and the continuing fantasy Della had had that she and Tanner Camden would still somehow have a happily-ever-after.

But Addie wasn't about to say that.

"You don't want Poppy anyway—I can tell," she said instead, bargaining. "So why push it? I *do* want her. I love her. The court has appointed me guardian, I've filed to adopt her. I can support her, raise her. I *want* to support and raise her. In her mind I'm her mom. In *my* mind, I'm her mom. You can't take her away." And just that quick Addie's throat clogged and tears flooded her eyes. Tears she furiously blinked back.

"But if I'm her father, that changes things. And I need to know," he reiterated but in a kind voice that made her all the more sure he'd seen what this was doing to her.

But whether or not he realized what was happening to her, Addie wanted him to know that she wouldn't take this lying down, so she squared her own shoulders and asked sternly, "And then what? How does it change things?"

"And then we'll just have to go from there."

Terrified that standing before her was the last straw, the straw that could break her, Addie knew there was nothing she could do to prevent him from going to court to request a DNA test. A request that she also knew the court would grant.

"Fine, have the test," she dared in a voice that pretended it wouldn't matter.

"I'll set it up ASAP," he said. Then he let that lay, pausing for a moment as if to give her a breather in all he was dumping on her before he said, "But since I'm the likeliest candidate for fatherhood... I took a three week leave, I've lost some days now getting here and tracking you down and I don't know how long it'll take to get DNA results. But since the clock is ticking on my time here I can't afford to waste any of it. I'd like to see her."

Of course he would. Damn him.

"And to maybe learn what it'll take if she *is* mine, because I don't know the first thing about babies," he added, giving Addie what she thought was a look at the tiniest crack in his armor.

Was that something she could use?

"It takes a lot," she warned, seizing the possibility and thinking about Sean's surprise over how much Poppy's care required. Thinking about how impatient and annoyed it had made him.

Which was when it occurred to her that maybe allowing Tanner Camden to experience all it involved to be a parent, to raise a child, might be her ace in the hole. It had scared off one guy. Maybe it would scare off this guy, too. Especially when he hadn't given the impression that he was overjoyed at the prospect of parenthood...

An idea began to take shape in her mind, giving her a small amount of hope...

"Where are you staying?" she asked him.

He obviously didn't understand the reason for the question but he answered anyway. "With my grandfather, out at the farm."

"And how would you rate yourself as a handyman?"

Because why not kill two birds with one stone if she could, now that she vaguely recalled something else from the time he'd dated her sister.

"I worked construction growing up—I can do just about anything that needs to be done by a handyman," he answered, again as if he was curious as to why he was being grilled.

But since he'd confirmed what she'd remembered, she forged on.

"Babies need care twenty-four hours a day," she said then, once more with some challenge to it. "If you really want to know what it takes to care for a baby, that's what you need to put into it."

"Okay…" he said tentatively.

"My grandmother's old house—the one you think isn't livable? Poppy and I have needed to move into it and it *does* need a lot of work. If you really want to learn what it is to be a dad, I'll trade you childcare lessons for help with the house. Poppy and I have rooms upstairs, but downstairs there's a bedroom and another bathroom—if you can get it working. You could use those and stay with us."

Tanner Camden stared at her for a moment, another frown on that handsome face, as if he was wondering what she had up her sleeve.

Then he said, "You're not worried about inviting a strange man to live with you?"

"You're not completely strange," she said somewhat disparagingly, causing a faint smile to cross his lips. "And I'm not a kid anymore, I can take care of myself, so if you have any ideas about getting near me you can let them go here and now. Plus, I know your family, I know *of* you—I've heard your grandfather bragging about what a hero you are, so I don't suppose I have to worry. And if you step out of line I'll call Ben and tell him."

That took the faint smile into a full one. Which only raised the appeal of his good looks. "You'll call my grandfather and squeal on me?"

"In a heartbeat."

"Well, that *is* a threat," he said facetiously.

No matter how amusing he might be finding this, Addie was still all business. "So unless you're afraid of living with me—"

He laughed. "I am but I think I can get through it." More facetiousness.

Addie ignored it. "Then we have a deal?" she said with far more bravado than she was actually feeling.

Again his gaze stayed on her, seeming to assess her before he said, "Okay, sure. When do you want me?"

She didn't *want* him. She had no desire to have another man around and certainly not one who posed a threat to her keeping Poppy. She just wanted the opportunity to bring home to him that parenthood was not a breeze—especially the diaper duty and sleepless nights that Sean had had particular problems with. And she wanted—needed—free help with her grandmother's house.

"Tomorrow," she decreed.

"Then tomorrow it is."

"Do you have a cell phone?"

"I do."

She held out her hand for it and when he gave it to her she put her number in it.

"Now you can just call rather than track me down…in case you change your mind and just want to go back wherever you came from and forget this."

Please do that…she silently beseeched from behind the stronger front she was faking.

"Tomorrow," was all he said, turning on his heels to go back to his truck.

And leaving Addie fearing that of all the bombshells that had dropped on her life this last year, the one Tanner Camden had just landed had the potential to be the worst.

Chapter Two

"You're kidding, right? You had a blind spot when it came to Della Markham when we were kids. I get that, I did some stupid things at that age, too. But you let her play you again less than a year ago?"

"Looks like it," Tanner said flatly to his older brother Micah. Their grandfather, Ben Camden, hadn't yet chimed in even though he was sitting at the kitchen table, too.

At Micah's request, Ben had fixed the three of them a big Sunday breakfast. Micah had said he had news—the previous weekend he and Lexie Parker had patched up all their old differences, Micah had proposed, and Lexie had accepted.

Lexie was off delivering the same news to her grandmother and aunt.

Tanner and Ben had done a round of congratulations, and after a little talk about how Micah had managed to win over his high school crush after all these years and a whole lot of murky water under the bridge, Tanner had announced that he was moving in with Addie Markham. And why.

Tanner's news had definitely altered the tone of the breakfast.

"No wonder you've been so closemouthed about why you showed up on leave out of the blue," his grandfather said somberly.

Tanner had been dodging their questions since his surprise arrival a few days earlier. He hadn't been in any hurry to own up to spending the night with Della Markham eleven months ago. Especially since he'd regretted it by the morning after. But since talking to Addie yesterday, he knew there was no way to deny it now.

"So there's really a baby this time and it honestly could be yours," Micah said.

"Yeah," Tanner answered curtly, staring at his own hand around his coffee cup.

"I thought that girl was unhinged when she was a teenager," Ben contributed.

To teenage Tanner, teenage Della had seemed just like most other girls he'd known. She'd thrived on drama, acted overly sensitive, and made big deals out of things he hadn't thought were big deals. It was all just the way girls were.

Only, instead of mellowing, Della's behavior had gotten worse during the three years they had dated.

Until yes, what she'd ultimately done *had* gone to an extreme and caused a fiasco in both their lives seventeen years ago.

But he meant it when he said, "She honest-to-God seemed like she'd finally grown out of all that... drama she'd liked so much."

Until the morning after that night in Billings, when she'd shown him she'd just done a damn good job of hiding it...

"When I was in town eleven months ago, I ran into her. It wasn't like she was looking for me or following me or anything—it really seemed like we ran into each other the way you run into everybody around here. We just had coffee. She told me what I know now was a pack of lies, but at the time it felt like she was through being...everything she'd been as a teenager. And I'm not who I was then. You aren't, either, Micah—"

"I can't argue that," his brother conceded.

"She said the reason she wanted to have coffee was to apologize for what she pulled after graduation," Tanner continued. "I really thought she'd moved on, done well for herself, and that she genuinely had her head on straight. And after coffee we went our separate ways without her even suggesting that we ever see each other again. If she'd tried to start something back up, I might have gotten suspicious, but the whole thing was just...nothing."

He shook his head, thinking back on every detail, asking himself for the hundredth time what he might have missed.

But he couldn't come up with a single thing.

"If I'd seen her even a second time while I was in town a red flag might have gone up for me," he went on. "But that didn't happen, so when our paths crossed again in Billings…" He shook his head once more, disgusted with himself for having been so gullible even as he was defending himself against it. "Honest to God, it just seemed like a coincidence. Especially since the night in Billings wasn't the original plan, it was a *change* of plans," he reminded the two men.

"A change of plans that everybody in town heard about," Ben pointed out.

"And might have given her the idea to follow you and make it *look* like a fluke that you ran into each other," Micah added.

Tanner conceded to that with a shrug.

"You had dinner and that led to a just-for-old-times one-night stand," Micah went on. "Okay, but—"

"Condoms were used," Tanner said, assuming that was going to be his brother's next question.

Condoms that he'd made sure to run down to the hotel's gift shop to buy, when things were heating up. But from there?

Della had made a sexy show of tearing them open with her teeth.

Della had put them on him.

Della had taken them off and disposed of them.

So he had no idea if one—or more—had failed…

Or, hell, she could have somehow stashed them,

taken the contents and used it to inseminate herself at some clinic or something...

Okay, maybe he was getting paranoid.

But with Della almost anything was possible.

He just wanted to kick himself for being so damn stupid and falling into bed with her again.

Ben had told them all about the birds and the bees when they were kids and the whole time he'd given the spiel his face had been crimson. It was that color now. "Any sex, no matter what you do, could still do the trick," he said, a warning he'd given during the initial talk years ago. "The bottom line is, if you spent the night with Della Markham, the baby she had nine months later could be yours," he concluded to get them past the subject of condoms.

Neither Tanner nor Micah said anything to that.

But Tanner could tell by his grandfather's tone what was coming next, because Ben had said it years ago to warn them that they would be responsible for the consequences of their actions.

"And if it's yours, you have to do the right thing," Ben added, meeting Tanner's expectations.

"*It* is a girl," he said, thinking of Addie's reprimand the day before for the same mistake. "A *girl* on top of it..." he lamented under his breath, thinking that he was all the more ill-equipped to handle that.

"Girl or boy, if you're the father, what does that mean for the future?" Micah asked cautiously.

Tanner just shook his head because he had no answer. The thought that he could be a father weighed almost more heavily on him now than it had the first time it had seemed like a possibility. When it came to his thinking about babies they might as well be space aliens.

He was all about his career. He was on the fast track and he hadn't thought about anything beyond that, let alone how to fit an infant—or even an older kid—into it. He just felt like he was in over his head with this…

"First things first," he said. Things were more manageable if he took them one step at a time.

"Yeah, let's not lose sight of the fact that it *is* possible the baby isn't yours. And if it isn't, then you can just go on with your life," Micah said objectively.

That note of detachment was exactly the tone Tanner needed and he ran with it.

"I'll have the baby's DNA and mine tested, and in the meantime I'm swapping work on that wreck of a house over on Spruce Street for lessons from Addie Markham on how to take care of a kid—"

"Like training for a mission so you're prepared for any eventuality," Micah interjected, his own years in the military giving him the same mindset.

"Right. This might be unorthodox but it should provide me with that."

This kind of back-and-forth with another military mind helped.

But something about that straightforward, businesslike, mission-oriented military tone seemed to rub their grandfather wrong.

"You watch yourself with Addie Markham," he

said, sounding protective of her. "She's not like her sister and she's had a bad last year and a half since her mom and dad got sick—they needed help and your Della wouldn't do it."

"She wasn't *my* Della," Tanner felt the need to correct.

"I'm just saying that that Della wouldn't lift a finger to help with her mom and dad," his grandfather persisted. "Addie moved in with them, worked and still took care of both parents. And she did it without a complaint and with no help—we all kept waiting for her sister to take a turn but she never did."

"You got to know Addie?" Tanner asked, confused about where this was coming from.

"I know her well enough now. Merritt's a small town—we all know who's who, what's going on, and the way things are. It was Addie alone who saw her folks to their graves when her sister wouldn't dirty her hands. And when that Della turned up pregnant without a husband and played at keeping a secret of who the father was—all the while walking around like some kind of celebrity, feeding off the curiosity and the talk her little mystery raised, and acting like some kind of prima donna—poor Addie did her best to tone it down, to keep a level head. Then it was Addie who stepped in with that baby the minute it was born, taking on that, too. You keep all that in mind, boy."

When the Camden boys were growing up, Raina Camden had been her sons' disciplinarian—a heavy-handed woman who hadn't tolerated weakness of any kind. Ben had been the softer voice of reason who had tempered their mother's intensity. So it was unusual to be presented with this sterner side of his grandfather.

Apparently, it shocked Micah, too. Eyebrows arched high, he spoke like a mediator. "Tanner isn't some horndog using this mess to score with the younger sister, Pops."

"I'm just saying," Ben said firmly, "that that Della was pretty enough to make a young boy over-look how unbalanced she was. I saw that, worried about it the whole time you had eyes for her—"

"Addie looks night-and-day different than her sister did," Tanner commented in case that might calm down his grandfather.

"That's the trouble—that Della was pretty but she was nothing compared to Addie Markham, and you better not let that strike a match with you. That girl has had enough, and now—for whatever reason that horse's patoot fiancé of hers took off—she's been put through more hurt. It's bound to have left some weak spots and you had damn sure better not use them to your advantage and hurt her any which way."

Ah… So Ben was remembering Raina's teach-ings about using others' weaknesses to one's own advantage…

Unfortunately, Tanner thought he'd already caused Addie some pain yesterday by just telling her he might be the father. He regretted it. But what was he supposed to do?

"It's a strictly hands-off arrangement," he assured

his grandfather. "She's already threatened to tell you if I step out of line."

"And if she does I'll take you down myself."

Tanner was four inches taller than his grandfather and marine-made-rock-solid. He dwarfed the much thinner, white-haired nearly-eighty-year-old. But with the way his grandfather said that, he believed him.

He made the gesture of surrender—arms up, palms out. "I'm not going near her."

Although Ben was right about her being prettier than Della.

Addie had been so much younger than he and Della that he hadn't taken much notice of her years ago—she'd just been the kid sister with stringy hair and braces that Della had sent away so they could make out.

But now?

The blond prettiness Della had possessed as a teenager hadn't tarnished with age, but it hadn't improved, either. Addie, on the other hand, had grown into a genuine beauty.

So much so that it was something he hadn't been able to overlook even under the circumstances of yesterday's encounter.

Her hair might have been pulled back but it was still a rich mahogany color shot through with dark reddish hues. She had luminous, peaches-and-cream skin, high cheekbones, the softest-looking pink lips, and big brown eyes sprinkled with gold dust that sparkled in them like glitter.

And her clothes hadn't helped—ripped jeans, a shirt tied around a small waist and just-curvy-enough hips, and a white tank top that she probably hadn't realized was cut barely low enough under her arms to show a tantalizing hint of side—

He yanked himself out of thinking about the outer swell of breasts that had somehow been on his mind when he'd gone to bed last night, too.

And again when he woke up this morning…

"Besides," he added, his hands down again. "I have enough going on. I won't make things any more complicated than they already are."

Not to mention that while his grandfather might be familiar with Addie's actions and have judged her a better person than Della, Tanner wasn't convinced that deep down Addie didn't have some of those volatile, unpredictable traits that—since Della—he'd avoided in women.

After all, he'd seen Addie go through a whole gamut of emotions the day before. First she'd been leery of him. Then she'd gotten riled over him referring to the baby as *it,* and more riled when he'd said he might be the father. From there she'd grown defensive and accused him of lying. Then he'd seen fear in her that had become outrage over birth control. Tears had come next, making those great eyes glisten when she'd tried to convince him not to pursue this.

And if that wasn't enough, she'd taken an abrupt turnaround in daring him to test the DNA, and topped that off with an attempt to scare him away before adding the cherry on top—her sassiness when she'd suggested the deal he'd agreed to.

It had been a wild ride just watching her, so how could he *not* wonder if it was an indication that she might be a little *unhinged* herself?

And while his grandfather knew of the admirable things she'd done and had had no cause to take note of anything else, Tanner was particularly on the alert for signs of women who could be rollercoaster rides—something, as of the previous day, that he certainly couldn't rule out with Addie Markham.

Which, contrary to what his grandfather thought, was a great big turnoff for him regardless of how beautiful any woman was.

"Just make sure you're careful about what you're doing," Ben said. Then, back to the tone that had tempered Raina's fierceness, he added, "I am glad you'll be helping Addie get that old house in better shape. That's a good deed and she has one coming."

Tanner nodded, then gathered his own breakfast plate and as many serving dishes as he could carry to take to the sink as he said, "I'd better pack up and make the move, get this started..."

And hopefully find out in the process that he *wasn't* the father of that baby so he could go back to his real life free and clear—something he had the impression Addie Markham wanted, as well.

"Oh. You're here..." Addie said when she opened the front door of her grandmother's house—her house now. She'd been on her way out when she discovered Tanner just coming up the walkway from the street to the small two-story home.

"You said come today," he reminded her, his gaze taking in the house's peeling, dingy white paint and chipped black shutters that were supposed to neatly bracket the windows but were instead all partly hanging off.

Addie saw in his expression that he was dismayed at the shape of the place. But when he reached the covered front porch, he stopped short of climbing the three steps onto it, and as his gaze settled on her where she stood in the doorway, his handsome face was once again neutral.

It was barely ten on Sunday morning and he was dressed much the way he'd been the day before—boots, camo pants and a beige crewneck T-shirt that traced every muscle—this one sporting the letters USMC over the right pec. He was freshly shaved and smelled faintly of soap.

And being aware of the scent put her in the unfortunate position of liking it.

"I was just going to leave you a note," Addie informed him, holding up the envelope she'd been about to tape to the outside of the front door. Inside was a key, a note telling him to go in, and advice for him to get to work on the downstairs bathroom.

Which, along with the bedroom he'd be using, was now tidy because she'd spent until after midnight cleaning that.

And although she'd told herself that it served Tanner right to come into a disgusting mess, that she shouldn't make *anything* easy or comfortable for the person who could possibly take Poppy from her, the clean freak in her—as Sean had frequently called her—just hadn't been able to have someone come into her home, regardless of what a shambles it might be, and find the bedroom and bathroom he'd be using dirty.

"What does the note say?" he asked.

She opened the envelope, removed the key and handed it to him. "That's to the front door and the note says you should probably go in and work on the bathroom."

"You're leaving?"

Boy, did she wish he didn't smell so good! It actually drained some of the hurry out of her.

"Since it's the talk of Merritt, you've probably heard I was left at the altar last Sunday," she said, holding her head high and not letting a drop of defeatism or depression enter her voice. "The non-wedding was at Gloria's. When you found me yesterday, I was taking all the gifts out so I can return them next week. But I've left her backyard a mess for this whole time and I promised I'd use today to clean it up."

He raised his chin. "Is the baby inside?"

"No. I've had so much to do…" She hated telling him her business. But because he was thinking that he might have a claim to Poppy she supposed she had to explain some things to make sure that he knew she'd made arrangements for the baby to be cared for while she couldn't do it and that she was in no way shirking her duties.

So she went on to tell him briefly about the need to move out of her former fiancé's apartment, and to make her grandmother's house as move-in-able as she could—all of it in a hurry.

"My best friend, Kelly Harrison—you wouldn't know her because she moved to Merritt after you were gone—"

"*That* was the name of the friend I found out about yesterday. She's who finally gave me information that actually led to you."

Kelly hadn't mentioned him but they'd barely spoken last night.

"Kelly has been babysitting Poppy during the days so I can get everything done. It's a huge favor because she has her every day—and has offered to do that until I can get things under control—but there's just no other way I can do everything I need to do and give Poppy the care she needs, too. I usually have her with me overnight, but Poppy was fussy yesterday and she wore them both out. It seemed like the best thing for Poppy and for Kelly to just let Poppy stay the night last night, though. I went over early this morning to give her her bottle and have some time with her while Kelly went to church, and I'll pick her up this afternoon when I get Gloria's yard finished. But that's where Poppy is right now—at Kelly's."

He nodded, seeming to take it all in stride rather than take issue with it, to Addie's relief.

Then, bypassing the subject, he said, "What work needs to be done on the bathroom?"

"The toilet flushes but then won't stop running, and there's a little leak around the shut-off valve— I have a towel tied around it and a bucket under the towel. The showerhead is completely corroded, so I couldn't even get water to come out of it—that might be the only problem, but until it's changed I won't know."

"Okay, so how about we go to Miss Gloria's separately—you head there, I'll stop by the hardware store on the way. I can pick up a few quick fixes that I can do late tonight or first thing tomorrow morning that may take care of the bathroom problems. Then I'll meet you and help with the yard cleanup."

"The running toilet might keep you up all night if you don't get it done, and if changing the showerhead isn't enough you won't be able to shower," she warned to make it clear that no matter how inconvenient it might be for him, she wouldn't amend her rule that he slept downstairs and used only the downstairs bathroom.

"I've made it through worse, I'll be fine."

She'd given him the opportunity. If he passed it up, then what he had to deal with overnight was his problem. And if he didn't *mind* helping with Gloria's yard...

Addie considered the offer.

It wasn't part of their deal and it seemed a little strange to have some other man working with her to clear away the remaining evidence of her wedding that wasn't.

But the idea of getting closer to putting it behind her was appealing. And she also thought it was possible that with Tanner along, Gloria might curb some of the apologies and pity. *Anything* that distracted from well-meaning Gloria's mea culpas was hard to pass up.

And look at those shoulders, those biceps...it'll be like having a superhero's help...

That was a dumb thought, she silently reprimanded herself, even as she realized her gaze had drifted to his muscles.

And lingered.

And shouldn't have...

She yanked her gaze to his face again and said, "Okay. Thanks. I appreciate the help."

Then she moved out of the doorway to allow him entrance and added, "Come on, I'll show you where to put your things and then I'm ready to go."

Somehow her *ready to go* had sounded slightly insinuative. And coming after ogling him a little, she really wished it hadn't.

But there was no clue as to whether or not he'd caught it, so she chose to believe she alone had heard it and led the way straight down the hall that ran to the kitchen, stopping halfway to point to her right.

"That's the bathroom," she informed him. "Oh, and I forgot, when I went to put towels under the sink there's a drip under there, too. So there's another bucket inside the vanity and the towels are just on the shelf."

Then she pointed into the doorway directly across the hall to the left. "And that's the bedroom," she announced, going a couple of feet farther to allow him access without entering either room with him.

He followed to the spot she'd been in, leaned his head into the bathroom door, then looked into the bedroom.

"There's only a twin bed," Addie said as if he wasn't seeing that for himself.

A twin bed that was not going to be ample for his size. But as far as she was concerned, the less comfortable he was, the less sleep he would get. Add that to the sleep she intended to make sure he lost with Poppy's middle-of-the-night feedings and she'd have just one example of how difficult it was to be a parent.

"I did put on clean sheets last night, though," she told him. "And I got a new blanket and pillow on my way home this morning after feeding Poppy. Your clothes can go in the dresser drawers or the closet." Because she'd also cleaned those so neither the drawers nor closet would be musty.

Although maybe musty-smelling clothes were preferable to the pleasant scent of fresh man that she couldn't seem to stop appreciating.

"I'll just stow my gear in the closet for now and we can go," he said, disappearing into the room.

Addie used the time to put the Scotch tape back in a drawer and throw away the envelope with the note to him in it. Then they headed out to their respective vehicles and went in opposite directions.

It only took Addie five minutes to get to Gloria's house and she was grateful that her mother's friend was still at church when she arrived so she could merely go through the side gate into the backyard.

Oh, Gloria, this is what you've had to look at all week? she thought when she stopped just inside the gate and surveyed the yard she hadn't been in since the Monday before.

The ordinarily impeccable space was in a very sad state, with the decorations put up by Addie and Kelly having deteriorated.

And the sight of it all caused the feelings that Addie had been outrunning the last five days to wash over her now.

She was hurt, yes. But that was actually the least of it.

She was angry, too.

And so...oo embarrassed—all the more when she pictured the wedding guests who'd been here last Sunday.

Plus, there was no denying that her confidence was a little shaken. Sean had pursued her from the first moment he'd moved to town. He'd boosted her ego with praise and adoration that she guessed had gone to her head. Praise and adoration that, in the end, had blinded her because never—ever—would she have guessed that he would end up doing what he did.

But here, at the site where she could have become

Mrs. Sean Barkley, she couldn't deny she also felt a secret sense of relief.

And guilt for that relief...

"Just get this done, Ad," she advised herself, heading for Gloria's garage.

The garage's rear door opened into the backyard and just inside was Gloria's ladder and an extra-large empty trash barrel. After carrying out the ladder and then rolling out the trash can, she retrieved the box of plastic trash bags she'd brought for the occasion.

She wanted to be able to get as much as possible in each bag. She'd arranged with Gloria's trash company to pick up the extra refuse that would be added to Gloria's usual amount, but they were charging Addie for each additional bag. So she needed to fill them as fully as she could in order to keep the number to a minimum.

With that in mind she lined the barrel with one of the bags, nearly falling in headfirst in her attempt to get it to the very bottom.

Then she moved the trash can to the white carpet runner that she'd laid on top of the stepping stone path that led out to Gloria's gardens. And to the platform where the ceremony was to have been performed with the gardens as the backdrop.

She paused at the starting point, not eager to set foot on the runner.

It was to have been the aisle she walked down.

It had been the aisle she'd walked alongside of at the rehearsal on Saturday.

And she suddenly had a sharp image of Sean at the other end of it, watching for her, smiling at her...

You stood down there and watched me come, went through the whole rehearsal, and never let on...

How could he have done it the way he did it?

Why couldn't you have just said you wanted out? Why did you have to make it a spectacle? Make me a spectacle?

"Hi, honey."

It was Gloria's voice that interrupted her thoughts, catching her stalled at the starting line, staring down that aisle.

And once again there was pity in the older woman's tone. Pity in her expression when Addie glanced at her standing on the threshold of the sliding glass door she hadn't heard open.

Oh no...

"Hi," she greeted cheerily to counteract the impression she was certain she'd given Gloria.

It didn't help.

"You're thinking about how you were going to walk down that carpet to your groom, aren't you?" Gloria said sympathetically.

"No," Addie lied. "I was wondering if it would be easier to roll it up or let it stay so I can drag the trash can on it."

Gloria nodded compassionately, humoring her by pretending to believe her. "Probably leave it down," she suggested. "Unless it bothers you..."

"Nope," Addie said, stepping fearlessly onto the

runner and pulling the trash barrel to position it there, too. "Thanks for bagging up all the plates and utensils and glasses and things," she said with a nod at the unused plasticware.

"I wanted to keep it all clean for you and it was the least I could do…"

Here we go…

Addie changed the subject fast. "Tanner Camden will be here any minute. He's going to help so I can get everything cleared out today, and then you can finally be done with all this."

"I haven't minded," Gloria assured her. "You don't even have to do it today if you're not up to it. I want you to take whatever time you need because I'm so, so, sor—"

Tanner came through the gate just then and Addie thought, *Saved by the Marines*! because the moment Gloria spotted him, she went from looking pityingly at Addie to beaming at the big marine.

"Tanner! Good morning!"

"Miss Gloria," he responded.

"Oh, stop the *Miss*," she said coyly. "I'm not the librarian anymore and you aren't a little boy."

"Gloria," he amended at her request and Addie had the distinct impression that the older woman loved hearing him say her name.

"Been to church, I'll bet," he added—obviously taking his cue from her Sunday-best dress and the small pillbox hat she was wearing over her salt-and-pepper bob.

He went on to ask how the service had been—

generally the talk of every Sunday—and Addie used their exchange to take the trash can down the aisle while she could do it without scrutiny.

About the time she reached the platform she heard Gloria say, "I know what! I'll change out of my dress, boil some eggs, and we'll have egg salad sandwiches for lunch—the three of us, out here on the patio. How does that sound?"

Better than more sorrys, Addie thought. But even though the suggestion was made to Tanner, she called from the distance, "Don't go to any trouble."

"No trouble," the older woman insisted. "I'm happy to have something to do since my back won't let me help with all this."

"If we're talking about the egg salad that won you a blue ribbon that sounds good to me," Tanner said as if it would be a treat.

Addie hadn't known him to be so smooth when he was a teenager. But she was grateful that somewhere along the way he'd developed a bit of charm and that it managed to curb Gloria's cloying commiserations.

"I'll get busy," the former librarian announced, hightailing it inside.

Addie stepped onto the platform, turned and pulled the empty trash can up after her, catching sight of Tanner as he looked around with an eye toward what needed to be done.

There was the stagelike platform itself—sheets of plywood painted white, raised on cinderblocks that were hidden behind the satin skirt nailed to the edges of the wood. Multiple trees were strung with white globe lights and strings and strings of additional lights over numerous limbs up to Gloria's house, forming an incandescent ceiling.

There was another sheet of painted plywood that had held the sound system and, near to that, a ring of ground lights that marked where the dancing was to have occurred—solar ground lights on spikes that Gloria had taken a fancy to so Addie had promised she would reposition them around the borders of the yard after the wedding as thanks. A myriad of folding tables also needed to be put away.

Once he had taken it all in, Tanner focused on Addie and the platform, and said, "So this first, huh?"

His tone was businesslike, as if he was tackling just any old job, and that was how Addie answered.

"This arch thing has to come down. All the decorations can go into the trash. The poles themselves are fence posts—those Gloria is going to use as an edge to her vegetable garden, so they can go over there..." Addie pointed to the plot in the corner of the yard where a few vegetables were sprouting in rows.

"The McKenzies down the street want the plywood that I used to make the dance floor," she continued in the order in which she planned to dismantle and dispose of everything. "They said to just leave it on the side of the house and they'll send their son to get it. They want the cinderblocks underneath the plywood, too—their daughter is getting married in two weeks and they want to do this same setup. Hopefully it won't pass on any bad luck."

Looking beyond the platform, she said, "Then we can deal with the tables. All the stuff on them will go home so I can use it and it doesn't go to waste. Well, all but the napkins. Gloria is taking those... I don't know why she didn't when she bagged everything—"

"She just wanted napkins?" Tanner asked.

"They're monogrammed...names, date... It was her idea. She said then I wouldn't have to look at them and be reminded." And Addie hadn't argued.

"The tables themselves are Gloria's and go in the basement," she went on. "And then whatever else needs to be cleaned up once the big stuff is out of here. You saw how the front yard looks—this, back here, was just as perfect before, and I need to leave it that perfect again," she finished.

Tanner nodded. "Okay. Let's get to work," he said, joining her on the platform and going to one pole while Addie went to another.

For a fair amount of time they worked without saying anything that didn't apply to the job at hand. But all the while Addie could feel Tanner watching her covertly and wondered if he was noticing that she wasn't strictly dressed for work.

But so what if she'd felt like French-braiding her hair this morning and putting on jeans that didn't look like they were ready for the rag bag?

So what if rather than the old tank top and ratty

shirt she'd had on yesterday, today she'd opted for a pink V-neck T-shirt that fit correctly?

And so what if—for the first time since last Sunday—she'd used a little eyeliner, a little mascara, a little blush, a little lip gloss?

She was just tired of looking like someone who had been left at the altar, and had decided before she'd gotten out of bed this morning that it was time she showed everyone that she was back to her old self and that there was no need for their pity.

In fact she'd asked herself why she hadn't thought of this earlier. Why it hadn't occurred to her that she might have been at fault for some of that pity that had been doled out because she hadn't presented a perkier front.

But one thing was for sure—putting more effort into her appearance had nothing to do with the knowledge that she'd be seeing Tanner Camden again. It had nothing to do with the fact that he'd been on her mind the whole time she'd cleaned the bedroom and bathroom for him, still when she'd gone to sleep, and again the minute she woke up this morning.

But what if he *thought* he was the reason?

He'd better not.

Just as that was running through her mind, he said, "So… I was a little afraid you might be kind of…bummed out…doing this. It can't be easy for you, can it?"

Oh.

So not only wasn't he taking credit for her looking better—if he'd even noticed she did—he was keeping an eye on her with the idea that this could be difficult for her.

That was nice...

Especially since it came matter-of-factly and free of any signs of sympathy.

"I'm fine," she answered with her standard answer this week.

"Really?" he said, as if he didn't see how that was possible. "One week from...all this not panning out—" he motioned with his chiseled chin to what surrounded them "—and you're fine?"

"I'm a lot of things," she responded ambiguously because she wasn't about to confide in him all that she was feeling. "But what's done is done and..." Okay, so her voice had faded out and gone suddenly weak. It *wasn't* easy being back in the middle of the scene of the crime. Or talking about it.

She took a breath to put the strength back in her voice, shrugged her shoulders and said philosophically, "I'm getting on with my life."

"Just like that?"

"Just like that," she confirmed decisively.

"It sounds like you might mean that." He dropped the sash, ribbons and dead flowers from the pole he'd been working on into the trash can and moved to the third post to begin dismantling it. "Is that because you weren't left at the altar by the love of your life?" he said as if he couldn't think of any other reason.

Sean, the love of her life?

No, she couldn't say that.

And she wasn't proud of the fact that she'd been about to *marry* someone who wasn't.

But again, she wasn't going to tell that to Tanner Camden, so instead she said, "Sean and I had been together for a long time and we were…comfortable. Companionable. We had a lot in common. Everyone said we were like two peas in a pod."

"But he wasn't the love of your life," Tanner persisted.

She'd unwrapped the pole she was working on and went to deposit the ribbons, fabric and dead roses in the trash can, too.

Rather than confirm or deny his assumption, she pointed at the bases of the poles and said, "Under those dead flowers are Christmas tree stands to hold the posts up. I'll keep one of them, Kelly wants one, and Gloria said she could use a new one, too."

But as Addie returned to her pole, she was still thinking about her reasoning behind accepting Sean's proposal, and out of the blue she said, "I know people who have—and have had—great marriages based on friendship, on comradery, and on the harmony they have with each other. I thought what Sean and I had was a good foundation."

"Friendship, comradery, harmony…" Tanner echoed. "That sounds…practical. But is practical good enough?" he asked skeptically.

She'd convinced herself that it was. But she said, "Apparently not for Sean…"

And there was a bite to her voice this time that made it obvious Tanner had hit a nerve.

"Sorry," he said.

He was probably apologizing for going too far, but after the week she'd just put in, that wasn't how she took it.

"Do *not* feel sorry for me," she ordered him. "I can't take another ounce of it from even one more person!"

Why that caused a small smile to tease his lips she didn't know, but it did. It also put a hint of humor in his voice when he said, "Yeah, I heard a lot of *poor Addies* when I was asking around about where to find you."

"I'm sure," she grumbled. "It's been one pity party after another and it's driving me right up the wall!"

That exclamation caused her to put a little too much oomph into unscrewing the last bolt of the tree stand, and rather than standing firm, the wooden post tipped precariously.

Luckily, Tanner was near enough to catch it in one big hand before it hit her.

Without saying anything, he took it out of the stand and carried it to the vegetable garden.

When he returned he said, "Okay, *Poor Addie*, why don't you take off the skirt thing around this floor while I finish these other two posts so you don't end up beaned in the head."

That *Poor Addie* had come with a bit of a goad. She preferred that, so she took it without comment and stepped off the platform to begin removing the satin that hid the cinderblock base.

But she did feel inclined to add, "It isn't that I don't appreciate that everyone cares. That they're being kind. At this point they probably don't know what else *to* say to me. It's just that—"

"You don't want to be Poor Addie," he finished for her.

"Because I'm *not* Poor Addie," she contended forcefully.

"So then…getting left at the altar… Did you have it coming?" Tanner asked as if he heard in her voice the question she'd asked herself all week.

But that was one more thing she wasn't opening up to him about, so she said, "Why would I have it coming?"

He shrugged his expansive shoulders. "Just asking. Maybe there was a wet and wild bachelorette party…"

"Oh, there was," she said. "Kelly and I opened a bottle of wine and took turns walking the floors with a crying baby, changing a lot of diapers, and called it a bachelorette party."

"That was it?"

"Kelly was taking Poppy while we went on the honeymoon. I didn't want not to be with Poppy any more than that. So no, I didn't have it coming to be left at the altar because I did something I shouldn't have done at a bachelorette party. I think other circumstances just set things off and then…"

And then was more than she wanted to get into,

so she altered course. "The way I look at it, if Sean was going to bail, better that he bailed before we were married than after. It just would have been even better if he'd done it in time to call the wedding off before everyone was here."

Tanner took another look around at the work yet to be done. "Your guests were all here?"

"Every one of them. Sitting in the folding chairs I took back to the rental shop Monday. With the music playing and the reverend waiting—"

"And you all dressed up, a beautiful bride..."

She wasn't sure if that was just the way he thought it should be phrased or if he was giving her a compliment.

She opted for *not* taking it as a compliment and said, "Yes, all of us were just expecting that Sean would get here any minute."

"Sean? The groom? I don't remember anyone around here named that."

"Sean Barkley—"

"As in Old Man Barkley who owned the jewelry store?"

"Old Man Barkley—Floyd—was his grandfather. When Floyd died Sean inherited the store and moved here from Wyoming. But Sean wasn't a jeweler so he turned the store into an office to sell insurance."

Tanner nodded, then backtracked. "And you were all waiting for him but he just never showed?"

"He'd had his bachelor party after the rehearsal the night before. Sean, his best man, and a few friends just went to the bar next to the gas station. I was told it didn't last long, that one by one his friends left, that when it came down to Sean and Trip, his best man, Sean told Trip to go ahead home without him even though Sean was supposed to spend the night there so we had that night apart. I guess Sean made Trip think he was coming to say good-night to me. When Sean never showed up at Trip's place, Trip thought we'd changed our minds and Sean had slept at home. Instead Sean had gone to Northbridge…to the wedding planner, to find out if she had the same feelings for him that he had for her. *That's* where he spent the night. He called me about an hour after the ceremony should have started, to explain it all. And to tell me that because Stephanie *did* have the same feelings for him, the wedding was off…" she said, unable to keep her tone pleasant. And unclear why she'd blurted the whole story out.

But now that she had, she'd opened the door for Tanner to say more.

"He didn't even tell you face-to-face?"

"No."

"And then did you have to come out and announce that the wedding was off?" Tanner said as if he hoped the answer was no.

"Kelly did that." While Addie had plopped down onto a chair in Gloria's guest room turned bridal dressing room to let the news sink in.

Minus any tears.

Shock giving way to the first of that relief…

"Kelly got everybody out," Addie went on. "Everyone except Gloria, of course, because it's her house—"

"And she's *still* feeling sorry for you," he guessed. *And regretting her part in it, too...*

But Addie had said enough, so she refrained from saying that. Instead she said, "Gloria was my mom's best friend. I think she sees herself as my surrogate mother since Mom died. But she's not like my mom was. My mom would have been sympathetic, but she wouldn't have...smothered me—"

Addie's voice cracked and a wave of grief, a wish that her mother, her father, her sister, had been here for her hit her hard and left her in need of a moment, before she said, "For sure there wouldn't have been any *poor Addie* in what my mom would have done. That wasn't her style."

"Yeah, I remember—she was the kind of person who didn't get flustered...even when she had good cause. Who didn't lose her temper... I appreciated that." His own voice dwindled slightly.

"Well, Gloria isn't anything like Mom. She's really touchy-feely. She's sweet but she *definitely* smothers—"

As if talking about her had conjured the older woman, Gloria poked her head out the sliding door just then and said, "The eggs are boiling. We're maybe an hour away."

"Can I help you do something?" Addie called back, feeling guilty now for saying anything that might seem critical of someone who tried so hard to be of help.

"Not a thing," Gloria assured before giving Tanner directions on the placement of the fence posts around the vegetable garden when she saw him headed there with the last of them.

That done, Gloria disappeared back into the house and Tanner returned to the platform.

"Gloria has been great, though," Addie said then. "I'm just…prickly, I guess."

With the platform cleared, Tanner took the trash can down and set it on the runner again.

"Seems like you're entitled to that," he allowed.

Addie took in a deep breath and exhaled. "But no more," she decreed. "It's been a week—"

"A *whole* week," Tanner joked.

"Long enough," she said firmly as she brought an armload of the platform's skirt satin to the trash.

"Okay…" he said with more amusement, as if he didn't believe he'd seen the last of it.

Addie decided she'd just show him rather than try to convince him as she dumped the cloth into the trash.

Then, remembering the price she would be charged for each bag, she bent over to press the contents as far down as she could to make room for more.

Unfortunately, she leaned in too far, and unlike when she'd initially put the bag into the trash can, this time she did lose her footing, and gravity took over.

Only Tanner's quick reaction kept her from falling all the way in when he grabbed her with both hands.

Both big hands that pulled her up and set her back on her feet.

And then stayed around her waist.

Great big hands that she could feel the strength of.

Great big hands that for some odd reason caused goose bumps to erupt on the surface of her arms.

And made her miss them when he finally took them away...

"Okay, it's probably better if we don't talk about any of this stuff so I can concentrate on what I'm doing," she said, looking up at that hella handsome face just above her.

Tanner nodded again, his extraordinary blue eyes peering into hers with what looked to be understanding.

And something else that she couldn't decipher.

It wasn't pity. Not at all.

In fact, it was kind of...a man-woman thing.

Then it was gone. His entire expression went emotionless and he stepped back.

Just as Gloria came out the sliding door again, carrying a pitcher of iced tea.

And ending whatever it was that had passed between them.

Chapter Three

"Oh, my sweet baby girl... I miss you so much when I'm not with you," Addie said to Poppy as she changed her diaper.

Addie had arrived at her best friend Kelly's apartment a little after five, just in time to do a diaper change while Kelly warmed Poppy's bottle.

The baby smiled at Addie and then proved she was hungry, by sucking mightily on her own tiny fist.

"Were you good for Kelly today?"

Kelly Harrison's one-bedroom apartment was tiny and Addie was changing the diaper on the sofa in the living room. Only a half wall separated the living room from the closet-sized kitchen, so Kelly could hear her and answered the question.

"She was good today. She must have had tummy trouble yesterday and it wore both of us out. But today she's eating fine and she's been bright-eyed and bushy-tailed again."

"Don't listen to that, Poppy, you don't have a bushy tail," Addie joked, nuzzling the infant's stomach with her nose once the dry diaper was fastened and before she re-snapped the baby's white romper.

Taking the warmed bottle from her friend, Addie settled in one corner of the couch to feed Poppy.

Kelly sat sideways on the opposite side of the sofa from her. "How'd you do on Gloria's yard?"

"Done!" Addie announced exuberantly.

"All of it? In one day?" Her friend sounded surprised.

Addie hadn't yet told her about what had happened with the burly marine who showed up yesterday.

"I had some help."

"Great! From who?"

"Well, you, sort of… You told Tanner Camden where to find me yesterday—"

"Oh… Yeah, I was so tired when I talked to you last night and in such a rush to meet Drew for church this morning that I forgot to tell you about the guy who came by yesterday. When I opened the door for a minute I thought it was that brewery guy—"

Since Kelly wasn't native to Merritt, she wasn't as familiar with everyone as Addie was.

"Micah is the brewery guy—he's Tanner's older brother. By a year," Addie explained. "Tanner is one of a set of triplets, but you're right, Tanner and Micah do look a lot alike even though Micah isn't one of the three."

"They're both *hott-tties*," Kelly concluded, drawing out the word for emphasis.

Addie would argue that to her, Tanner was even better-looking than Micah. But that wasn't relevant—or something she wanted to think about.

"Anyway," Kelly went on, "he told me his name and said he was looking for you. I recognized the Camden part of the name right off, so it seemed safe enough to tell him where to find you. Plus, I thought I remembered that *Tanner* was the first name of the guy your sister was with years ago—"

"Right. Tanner was Della's high school boyfriend. And apparently she was with him again eleven and a half months ago…" Addie filled in her friend on the reason why Tanner had been looking for her.

"Oh…" Kelly repeated, this time with worry in her tone. "Maybe I shouldn't have told him how to find you."

"He would have tracked me down eventually, one way or another—it's not like Merritt's a big city," Addie reassured her, realizing when Poppy squirmed in her arms that her hold on the baby had tightened slightly.

She eased up and leaned over to kiss Poppy's forehead as an apology for subconsciously hanging on a little harder when talking about the man who might have a claim to the infant.

"You don't really think he'd take her, do you?"

Kelly asked. "I mean, if he's a single guy in the military, what would he want with a baby? And if he's married or engaged or even has a girlfriend, he might not want the woman in his life knowing he slept with someone else. Or maybe the woman in his life won't want another woman's baby…"

For all Addie had thought about Tanner Camden during the last twenty-four hours, she somehow hadn't considered that he might *have* a woman in his life.

"There's no wedding ring," she said, thinking that she certainly would have noticed it if he wore one. "But beyond that, I don't know. I've really just been on the defensive since he showed up at Gloria's. At first I didn't believe Della had hooked up with him, so I took issue with that. Then I really balked when he said he might be Poppy's father—and thinking about him taking her…"

"Sure. That had to have upset you," her friend consoled when Addie's voice cracked.

"And then today…" Addie went on. "Well, today, it was *last* Sunday that was on my mind and I was kind of defensive about that, too. So I haven't actually asked anything about him or his personal situation. I just thought maybe I could scare him away by letting him see that taking care of a baby, raising a kid, might be more than he can handle."

Kelly nodded. "Shades of Sean…"

Addie told her friend about the deal she'd struck with Tanner as she set down Poppy's bottle, half-empty now, tossed the cloth diaper over her shoulder and repositioned the infant to pat her back in hopes of a burp.

"And it was Tanner who helped with Gloria's yard today?" Kelly asked, getting back to the beginning of this conversation.

"He showed up to move in this morning just as I was headed out to Gloria's. I was leaving a key and a note for him to go in so he could fix the downstairs bathroom, but he offered to do the yard instead. So I took him up on it. When we finished at Gloria's, he went back to the house to work on the bathroom—that's where he is now."

"I'm glad he helped get everything done at Gloria's so that can be over for you. And it's good that you'll have some help with the house, too," Kelly said as if she was trying to find a silver lining. "But what if he *is* Poppy's dad?"

"He can't have her," Addie said. "I'll fight him if I have to. I'll go to court and try to get custody—even though I know a biological father would have a better standing," she finished dejectedly because she knew that was true and that her chances of winning wouldn't be great.

"Maybe the DNA will prove he *isn't* her father."

"From your lips to God's ears..." Addie said, though without much hope.

"You don't think it's likely," Kelly guessed.

"As far as I know there weren't any other candidates for fatherhood in the last two years. And Della was so obsessed with Tanner...he was the standard she measured every guy by."

"I know you've said half a dozen times that for Della no one could hold a candle to him."

"Even when she was seeing a guy she seemed to really like, she would eventually say, *'But he still isn't Tanner.'* And every time a guy broke up with her she went right back to that—that the guy didn't measure up to Tanner anyway, so good riddance. And then she'd fall into a slump and start the fantasy all over again that she and Tanner *would* find their way to each other someday, and she'd decide it was better that she was available."

"I remember her saying that one night, when the three of us were having drinks. I thought she had to be drunk to think that after so many years and no contact she still might get back together with her high school sweetheart."

"She might have been drunk but it wasn't the booze talking. It was really what she wanted to happen." Addie had loved her sister dearly but Della had had a lot of issues. "Plus, she was so…oo happy about this baby. I didn't know if she'd found somebody who finally replaced Tanner—"

"But you were worried about that," Kelly interjected. "Because when she wouldn't tell you who the father was, you were afraid that if she *had* found somebody to replace the old guy it was a new obsession who might be already married…"

"And instead," Addie sighed, "maybe she just thought she finally had a way to rekindle things with her original obsession. I know she kept saying that her dreams were coming true, but—"

"It didn't occur to you that she'd actually hooked up with the high school boyfriend," Kelly finished for her. "I remember you were concerned that he was in town, but you said she told you they'd had coffee and that was it. And you were kind of keeping tabs on her, so you believed her when she said she hadn't seen him again."

"I *know* she didn't see him again in town, because I was more than kind of keeping tabs on her—I was watching her like a hawk. But sneaking away to trail him to Billings when I thought he was gone and we were in the clear? She could have done that. In fact, it would have been just like her. And I'm afraid that if there was any way to give herself even the smallest shot with this guy Della would have taken it."

Hearing the hearty burp Poppy let out, Addie took the baby off her shoulder and cradled her again. Looking down into that face that had somehow become everything to her, Addie literally went cold with the thought that she could lose her.

Kelly must have sensed that. "It'll be okay," she said as Addie coaxed the bottle back into the infant's mouth. "You're Poppy's mom now. He'll see that and unless he's a monster he won't take her away."

Addie could only shrug her shoulders in an I-hope-you're-right way.

Kelly's phone rang just then, and knowing it was likely Kelly's mother's daily call from Iowa, Addie said, "Take it. Tell your mom hello for me and I hope her cold is better."

"I'd call her back, but I do need to know how

she's doing or if I should get my aunt to take her to the emergency room to have her lungs listened to."

"Sure."

Kelly stood up, grabbed her phone off the ledge of the half wall and answered the call.

Not wanting to eavesdrop on her friend's conversation, Addie turned her thoughts to how much help Tanner had been today. He'd really done the work of two people, plus run interference with Gloria, so the cleanup had sailed along. And now it was all done, except the returning of the gifts, and she hoped she could start to work on putting Sean—and being left at the altar—behind her.

If only she could think that the *worst* was behind her…

But holding and feeding the baby, and talking to Kelly about Tanner, made the threat of him taking Poppy away from her fresh again. She told herself she couldn't lose sight of it—something she'd done today in the midst of contending with the remains of her misbegotten wedding.

Plus, she'd been under the influence of the pure potency of being around Tanner,

That hair, that face, those eyes, that body…

She was only human.

And watching all those muscles at work, having him volunteer to help with the chores Sean should have done, seeing him show some concern for how the chores affected her, the way he'd eased her embarrassment by teasing her a little about the *poor Addie* stuff topping it off by boosting her ego slightly with the *beautiful bride* comment...

Then adding to it all by saving her from falling into the trash can headfirst, with those big hands around her waist, hands that she could almost still feel...

And that look on his striking face when he'd set her on her feet again...

No, she hadn't been thinking about the threat he posed.

But she would from here on, she swore. She had to.

"Mom says hi back," Kelly announced, pulling Addie out of her reverie as she returned to the couch. "And her cold is better, thank goodness."

"I'm glad," Addie said.

"So this Tanner guy—" Kelly went right back to where they'd left off "—he *isn't* a monster, right? Those looks aren't deceiving, are they?"

"I was six years younger than Tanner and Della," she said after a moment. "And he was just my sister's boyfriend. It wasn't as if he and I had anything to do with each other, so I can't say I actually *knew*—or know—him."

"Sure," Kelly said.

"What I *do* know," Addie continued, "is that when he and Della were together I'd just started noticing boys myself and I *imagined* that Della had the kind of romance I wanted to have—I thought of them as the perfect couple, the football player boyfriend devoted to his cheerleader girlfriend. I thought he'd sweep her off her feet one day and carry her into the sunset where they'd live happily ever after."

Kelly laughed. "I had fantasies like that even without a big sister in love with some stud."

"But ultimately that's a long way from what happened. I came home from school early the afternoon Della told him she was pregnant," Addie went on. "Mom and Dad were out, so Della and Tanner were alone in the living room. I'd come in the back door, into the kitchen, and they didn't hear me. So I got close and then hid to spy on them, thinking I might see something juicy—"

"As any little sister would."

"But there wasn't anything juicy going on. Della was crying, telling him she'd taken a home test and she was pregnant," Addie said somberly. "And Tanner was *not* being her knight in shining armor…"

Recalling it made Addie cringe internally even now. "He was just sitting there, poker-faced. He wasn't being mean, but he wasn't saying not to worry, either. Or that she wasn't alone, or promising that he'd be there for her and the baby—"

"Any of the things that would have let him go on being the hero in the romance novel."

"He was just staring at Della…pale, like he was sick or something, all while Della was sobbing and telling him he couldn't leave her…*begging* him not to leave her…"

It was an ugly memory for Addie.

"And I know how it turned out," she said, "but

right then I felt so *bad* for Della. I hated him for what he *wasn't* doing. I couldn't stand to see what she was going through while he just sat there! I remember the only thing he did say was that he'd been accepted to the naval academy, asking her if she knew what a big deal that was…only thinking about himself…"

"Okay, that's not great. But they *were* only a week out of high school—they were just kids," Kelly said, weakly defending Tanner. "I imagine he was pretty shocked. And scared. You said he did eventually say he'd marry her…"

"Not that day," Addie said with some condemnation. "That day he just got up and walked out of the house, so I went in and calmed her down. She kept saying she knew he'd do the right thing but I wasn't so sure. Then, the next day she wanted me to go with her for moral support when she got him to agree to meet her in the park. That was when he finally did tell her he'd marry her but it was so obvious that it wasn't what he *wanted* to do—it was like he was walking to his own death. And after that I couldn't think of him as anything but a big selfish, self-centered jerk. Does that qualify as him being a monster?"

"I can see where it would leave you wondering about his character—"

"Oh yeah!" Addie confirmed.

"But on the sort-of-positive side," Kelly pointed out, "if he's a selfish, self-centered jerk who didn't want to mess up his future with a baby, maybe he'll still end up feeling that way. Maybe he's just here

hoping the DNA test will let him off the hook, and
if it doesn't, he probably won't want a kid interfer-
ing with his life any more now than he did when he
was a teenager."

"I'd like to think that," Clairy said. "But he did
come running the minute he heard about the baby
and Della's death—if it was out of a sense of responsibility, that could go against me. And if he came because he's just hoping for proof that he isn't Poppy's
father and then finds out he is and takes her? What if
he's still that detached, unemotional jerk I saw that
afternoon and I have to turn Poppy over to him?"
Addie said. "It could be like sending her out onto
an iceberg…or giving her to a robot. What kind of
life would she have?"

In the silence that meant Kelly didn't know what
to say, Poppy finished her bottle and Addie raised
her to her shoulder for another burp, tucking her
close to her neck as if that might keep the baby at-
tached to her, where Poppy would be well loved.

Unlike what the infant would be in for, Addie
was afraid, with Tanner Camden.

No, when Della had told him she was pregnant,
he hadn't reacted violently or in any way that had
made him a danger. He hadn't refused to take responsibility, or denied being the father, or called
Della names, or accused her of sleeping with anyone else.

But he also hadn't been caring or compassionate—qualities Addie felt were necessary in a good
father. Even when he'd agreed to marry Della he

hadn't so much as pretended that he was even re-motely happy about it. It had still been nothing more than an unwilling concession. And a stiff-backed, hands-off, clenched-teeth tolerance of Della's over-the-moon joy.

Witnessing it had made Addie incredibly uncomfortable. She'd ached for her sister for not recognizing how much Tanner *didn't* want her. Or the baby. For how disconnected he'd been.

And no, he hadn't gone along with Della's desperate pleas for them to elope immediately, without telling anyone about the pregnancy or the plan to marry.

And again Addie had hated watching her sister lapse into more sobs, more begging for him not to make them wait, not to bring parents into it, to just run off—something that Addie's young romanticism had also rooted for.

"It doesn't even make sense that he cares if Poppy might be his," she muttered, feeling again how much she'd hated Tanner on her sister's behalf. How much she'd gone on hating him even with all that had occurred after, "Maybe it's some kind of honor thing," Kelly postulated. "He hasn't actually *said* he wants to take Poppy and raise her, has he?"

Addie thought about that. "No, I guess he hasn't… He just kept saying that if he's her father he has to know."

"And you're going to show him what a big job it is to be a parent," Kelly reminded.

"Because it is," Addie said, feeling some hope return.

"He's probably just here out of a sense of obligation. Maybe if he *is* her father he'll pay some child support, figure he's doing his duty with that, and that'll be as far as it goes—except maybe a birthday or Christmas gift here and there."

"An absentee father," Addie said, not caring about Tanner's money but holding onto that renewed hope. And thinking that from what she knew of Tanner Camden it wasn't altogether unlikely.

"So maybe it will work in my favor that he's a cold fish," she said more cheerfully, hanging everything on the idea that that would be the case, that while he might have smoldering good looks on the outside, there might not be any warmth at all on the inside.

"Okay, my little sweetie pie, back to your own bed tonight," Addie said to Poppy as she carried the baby into the house after leaving Kelly's apartment. She placed the infant, still in the carrier portion of the car seat, on the wooden floor of the entryway, where she'd leave the seat until their next car ride.

She closed the door and took the diaper bag off her shoulder to set next to the carrier. Then she bent over to unbuckle the carrier straps and said, "But before we get to bedtime—"

"Hi."

Even though Tanner's truck was parked out front the sound of his voice startled Addie. She straightened up and spun around to find Tanner with one foot on the bathroom's threshold, the rest of him now out in the hallway that had been clear when she'd come in a moment before.

One look at him and she was at a loss for words.

Water had drenched an already-snug beige USMC T-shirt, giving it a little transparency and making it cling tighter to his muscular pecs, biceps and six-pack abs. Gloriously tighter.

Tanner seemed oblivious to the effect as he used a hand towel to dry his angular face where a five o'clock shadow had begun to sprout. Between the scruff and the wet-T-shirted torso, Addie's mind had gone blank.

"There's more problems in that shower than needing a new showerhead. Looks like the valve has been leaking, too—for who knows how long. Water was pooled in the head when I finally got it off—"

"And you got doused," Addie said, struggling to gather her wits before he realized she was ogling him.

"Yeah," he said. "I had to put the corroded showerhead back on until I can get a new valve, too, so I'll have to go out to the farm to shower. Thought maybe I'd bring back some Mexican food—do you like Mexican food?"

She was only half listening as she studied the breadth of his Atlas-like shoulders that really did look as if they could hold up the heavens.

Focus, Ad, focus...

Did she like Mexican food? Was that what he'd asked? "I do," she said, hoping she was right.

"Burritos? Enchiladas? Tacos? What's your pleasure?"

Her *pleasure*?

Oh.

There was quite a bit of it in just looking at him.

And why was she thinking about running her hands over all those muscles?

"Quesadillas? Tostadas?"

The sound of his voice suggesting other Mexican dishes helped her recall that food was the pleasure he was talking about.

"I like it all," she said weakly, still thinking more about what she was looking at than about what she wanted to eat. But she knew she had to stop that and said, "A cheese enchilada would be good."

Quit looking at him! she told herself sternly. *Remember how he was with Della! Remember that he could steal Poppy!*

So what if he was well-built and as hot as he could possibly be?

Poppy...think of Pop...

Poppy, who was still in the child carrier on the floor, the carrier he didn't even seem to have noticed.

Tearing her gaze off Tanner, Addie returned to what she'd been about to do when he'd greeted her—she bent over and unbuckled the tiny baby, picking her up.

"This is Poppy, by the way," she said then, her tone implying that he was negligent to have ignored the baby he was claiming might be his.

His eyebrows arched and the big strong Marine suddenly looked scared to death as he gazed in the direction of the infant in her arms.

"Hi…" he said feebly, as if he'd just been introduced to an adult he was wary of.

"Don't you want to hold her?" Addie asked just to further unnerve him.

He opened those massively bicepped arms, the towel in one hand, his other palm out in surrender. "I'm wet and grimy—I really need a shower."

"You could still look closer at her…"

He took one long-legged step forward, craned his neck and peered at the baby as if the mere sight of her was a lot for him to handle. "That's her, huh…"

"This is her," Addie confirmed.

"She's a… pretty baby, isn't she?" he asked uncertainly.

"I think she is."

"And she does look… healthy, sturdy…" He was clearly out of his element.

"She's doing well," Addie confirmed.

"But she's so tiny…"

"She's in the right percentiles for weight and length, making all her milestones—"

"So she's supposed to be that little…" Tanner said, exhibiting his cluelessness.

"She's just right."

He nodded. Then, as if he didn't know what else to say or do, he shied away and looked back to Addie who almost laughed at his skittish response and limited knowledge before he went on with what he'd been saying. "Okay, then… I'll take off so I can get back with the food," he said before he stood tall again, retraced that one step, and set the towel on the counter just inside the bathroom door almost sounding relieved, as if he'd jumped the first hurdle. "I'll see you in a little while."

Then he hightailed it around the two of them and went out the front door.

Addie leaned down to kiss Poppy's perfect forehead and whispered, "Maybe this was all it took to send him running…"

At least she could hope that was true.

While Tanner was gone Addie put the bouncy seat in her bathroom upstairs, strapped Poppy into it and took a quick shower to wash away the day's yard cleaning.

Once she had, she wasn't quite sure what to wear. If she was going to remain alone with Poppy she would have put on one of the oversize, ragged and faded T-shirts she usually slept in, and called it a night. But she wasn't going to be alone.

She was also determined not to dress as if she was about to have dinner with a sexy marine, so she settled on a pair of yoga pants and a white V-neck T-shirt, all the while talking to Poppy as if the infant was another adult helping make her decisions.

It was while she was brushing her still-damp hair that she took herself to task for being as blown away as she'd been by that earlier vision of Tanner. Addie reminded herself that he was still a threat, regardless of how good he looked.

But not even that reminder kept her from applying eyeliner, mascara and blush that she would not have ordinarily put on mere hours before bed.

Afterward, she gave Poppy a bath, put on the baby's pajamas and fed her a before-bed bottle. Tanner still wasn't back and it left Addie wondering if he might be dragging his feet to make sure the baby was already asleep when he got there.

And if that was the case, if he wasn't genuinely interested in Poppy and learning how to care for her, then why was he even here?

Maybe Kelly was right and this was just some kind of honor thing, a sense of obligation he felt. And if he proved to be Poppy's biological father, the most he might do was offer some child support that could make him feel as if he was contributing and he'd disappear once and for all.

"Keep your fingers crossed," she whispered to Poppy when she'd finished feeding her.

The baby was falling asleep in her arms by then, so Addie decided it was senseless not to put her to bed even though Tanner wasn't back to get any kind of bedtime instruction. She carried the infant upstairs to the bassinet, kissed Poppy's tiny temple, took the baby monitor with her and quietly left the nursery.

Tanner walked in the front door just as Addie was going down the stairs.

The jeans and fresh white T-shirt he was wearing were dry, he was clean-shaven again, and now he smelled like fresh ocean air—which was unfortunately even better than how he'd smelled this morning.

He was toting another duffel bag tucked under one arm, an enormous toolbox in one hand, and a take-out bag of food in the other, all of it leaving his biceps stretching the T-shirt's short sleeves nearly to the limit and again leaving Addie with an eyeful and basking in a scent that turned her insides to jelly.

Don't be fooled, she told herself to keep her perspective. *Don't forget how he treated Della, don't forget that he wouldn't get anywhere near Poppy a little while ago.*

"Is it okay that I just come in without knocking even when you're here?" he asked after the fact.

"That was part of what I was thinking when I gave you the key this morning—if I'm mid-diaper-change or feeding Poppy I can't answer the door, so you kind of need to."

He nodded. "Sorry it took so long—my grandfather messed up his computer and asked me to fix it before I left the farm. Then I got to the Mexican place just as they were about to close, so they didn't really want to do another order. I had to talk them into it."

Addie pretended to accept his excuses but she wasn't convinced that he hadn't merely dragged things out to avoid Poppy and doing what he was actually supposed to be here doing.

"I can take the food while you do something with the other stuff," she offered, reaching for the sack.

"Yeah, I brought some tools this morning but after looking at this place I decided I'd better borrow my grandfather's. A lot of work needs to be done around here."

If not I might not have agreed to this deal, Addie thought. But she didn't say it; she merely took the bag of food into the kitchen.

The house was sparsely furnished by what little Addie had put into storage from her family home and Della's apartment, including her own double bed and bureau, and the single bed and dresser that were in the room downstairs that Tanner was occupying. The kitchen contained the only piece of furniture that had originally belonged to her grandmother—a very old, round, badly scarred, dark oak pedestal table.

Because the chairs that went with it had all had missing rungs and broken or splintered backs and seats, they'd had to be discarded. Until Addie could replace them, Gloria had loaned her two old ladder-back chairs that didn't match the kitchen table.

"Water, iced tea or lemonade?" she called to Tanner, depositing the bag on the table and moving to the refrigerator for drinks.

"Thanks but I brought beer. I'll have one of those and you're welcome to them, too," he answered from the bedroom, appearing a split second later with a six-pack he'd had stashed either in the second duffel bag or the toolbox, because Addie hadn't seen it before.

"No, thank you, I think I'll stick with water." *Which won't diminish my capacity to remember why you're here no matter how good you look or smell...*

Tanner joined her then. Holding the six-pack aloft, he said, "Can I put this in the fridge?"

"That and anything else. If you're staying here you have run of whatever you need to have run of," she told him. "You don't have to ask."

He put the six-pack in the refrigerator and then brought one bottle to the table.

"Glass?" Addie asked from her position at the cupboard next to the sink.

"No, thanks, the bottle is fine."

Addie filled one for herself with purified water from a pitcher. When she got to the table he was unloading the bag.

"I got you the enchilada dinner—it has three of them, rice and beans, too. You worked hard today. One enchilada isn't enough to keep an ant alive," he explained.

"I am starving," she confessed.

"I'm having the smothered burrito platter but I got a side of extra green chili in case you might want some of that, too—there's triple-X-spicy green on the burrito, but the side is mild because I didn't know how much hot you could take."

She wasn't too sure herself...

But not in terms of food.

"I don't like things too spicy," she said.

"And there's guacamole and salsa and chips to share." He sat on the chair she'd left for him, took a swig of his beer, tried the burrito and told her it was great but still milder than he liked.

For a few minutes they ate in uncomfortable silence. Then, as if they were strangers seated at a wedding reception he asked, "Have you been in Merritt all this time or did you leave and come back?"

"I was in Billings four years for college. Then I moved back," Addie answered in the same wooden manner.

"Small towns—people either love them and can't wait to get back, or can't wait to leave them and never come back," he said as if it was just something to say.

"It's home," Addie said simply. "It's where my mom and dad and Della were, so it's where I wanted to be, too…wherever my family was."

The family she'd lost now. Except for Poppy.

Whom she might lose in the near future…

That thought raised Addie's stress level but she tried to keep it under control and continue the awkward conversation he'd begun. "I guess, given what you think of small towns, you're one of the ones who couldn't wait to leave and never come back."

"I couldn't wait to leave—"

"To get away from Della," she accused, some of that stress making her speak before she'd thought better of it.

Tanner arched his eyebrows in a way that didn't

deny the accusation but then said, "I couldn't wait to leave so I could get started doing what I'd always wanted to do—go to Annapolis, join the Marines. Doing what I do makes it hard to come back, but when I do I'm glad to see family, old friends..."

Was that what he'd considered Della—just an ordinary old friend whom he could have a quick, no-ties, one-night-stand with? While Della had no doubt felt she was getting a second chance with him?

Be nice...she told herself. Now was her chance to learn more about him, not alienate him.

"I'm sure Ben is glad to have you home whenever you can get here," she said.

"He is. But I talk to him by phone as much as I can. We email, video-chat—I keep in touch."

Addie nodded. She supposed he got points for making that effort. Maybe that could be the extent of his fatherhood, too...

Another silence fell before he said, "So just college and back to Merritt for you..."

"Right. I almost didn't even go away for that. The older I got, the closer Della and I became, and I considered skipping college, working at the bank with her. I thought we'd each get married, have and raise kids here, together—you know, babysit for each other, take family vacations, have holidays..."

Addie suffered a stab of pain at the recollection of how she'd thought things would be, but she took a bite of rice to buy herself a minute to put those plans, those dreams behind her—the only place for them now.

Then, more pragmatically, she said, "Ultimately I figured we'd still get to all that if I took four years out to get my degree, so I did. But even if I had gone away for more than that I would have had to come back to Merritt..." She couldn't keep sadness from her voice.

"To take care of your folks," Tanner filled in. "My grandfather told me about you moving in with them for that."

"A year and a half ago Dad had a horrible heart attack that he just couldn't bounce back from, and Mom developed COPD that got so bad she had to be on oxygen. She got winded just walking from her bed to the bathroom, so she couldn't take care of Dad or the house or the cooking or anything."

"What about Della? Or did you get a degree in nursing so it was more up your alley?"

"My degree is in elementary education—I teach kindergarten," she said before she cautiously added, "But no, Della wasn't really up for caretaking sick parents with me living here or not."

In fact Della had flat-out refused; she'd said it was all too ugly for her, that she didn't want that in her life...

"I mean, she did whatever I asked her to," Addie added defensively. "She picked up prescriptions or ran errands. But she didn't have the stomach for anything hands-on with Mom or Dad."

"She must have had to cook and clean for herself... Didn't she do that for them to share the load?"

"Della..." Addie wasn't sure how to explain

the situation without making her sister sound bad. "Della sort of needed to live in her own world to be happy. I knew that about her. It was just better for all of us if she didn't have to deal too much with Mom and Dad going downhill," Addie concluded.

"So you had to do everything?"

"I wanted to take care of them," she said honestly. "To me…it gave me the chance to spend as much time with them as I could before I lost them." An opportunity she hadn't had with her sister because Della's death had been so quick and unexpected.

Thinking that brought a wave of grief again.

She didn't know whether Tanner saw it or not but for a moment he didn't interrupt the silence she left. Then he changed the subject.

"So you teach kindergarten, huh?" he said. He'd finished his meal and made a large dent in the guacamole, salsa and chips, and now leaned on his forearms, his hands around his beer bottle.

"I do," Addie confirmed, grateful for what seemed like safer territory.

Then it occurred to her to use the new topic to her advantage and she said, "It's been the perfect job. Not only do I love working with kids, but it was great when I was taking care of Mom and Dad. I could go home during lunch and recess when my aide watched the kids, and then get back home again by three thirty or four in the afternoon when school let out."

"I'm sure that did help."

"And when Della…" There was no way to put

it that didn't stir another wave of grief in Addie. "When Poppy became mine my principal got me maternity leave *and* family emergency time to bring Poppy home and get everything taken care of. That took me into summer vacation, so I've had the last two and a half months with Poppy. Now I'll have until mid-August with her."

"That would be more than the military would give," he said as if he'd caught that she was high-lighting her own advantages for childrearing.

"Even once school starts again," she continued running with it, "Merritt's best day care is right next door to the school, and they take infants and go all the way through preschool. Plus, what worked out with Mom and Dad is still the case—my workday doesn't start too early and I'll be able to leave by mid-to-late afternoon. And there's fall break, Christmas and spring breaks, a lot of holiday days off, and every summer. Also, my job is understanding and lenient when it comes to needing to take time when your child is sick."

Maybe she'd given too much of a hard sell, because Tanner didn't say anything when she'd finished.

But what *could* he say, she asked herself—that she had convinced him Poppy was better off with her, so forget the DNA test they'd discussed setting into motion first thing tomorrow morning while working on Gloria's yard, and he'd just be on his way?

Then, in a quiet voice, he said, "I know how you feel about the baby."

She merely raised a protective-mother-bear chin at him.

He didn't repeat himself, either, but Addie could hear his response anyway. Regardless of what Poppy meant to her, he had to know if he was Poppy's father. Even if he was unprepared for that turn of events in his life.

"I'm not looking to hurt you, Addie," he said softly, the air of forced small talk gone as those blue eyes peered into hers, his expression telling her that he meant it, but that he was bound to this course he'd set them on.

The way his eyes held hers made her feel a little flushed. And her capacity to remember that he was a threat did seem diminished as she got a little lost in that face that was just too handsome.

She took a breath to shore up her defenses and reminded herself that there was some information she needed to have about him.

In a businesslike tone, she said, "Are you married? Do you have a girlfriend or a fiancée or someone who would help with a baby?"

He shook his head. "I'm not married and no, there's no girlfriend or fiancée or anyone."

Good!

But only because it reinforced her plan to discourage him. Not because she cared if he was single or not.

"So no help," she concluded as if that said it all and gave her another small victory.

"I do have a buddy in my unit who has a kid.

Wayne's wife and kid live on base. Last year another buddy of ours was deployed at the same time
his wife was and Wayne's wife Linda took their two
year old while they were gone…"

It was obviously not a firm plan, just something
he was mulling over. But it was enough to let her
know that he'd seen through her attempt to estab-
lish that his situation didn't accommodate Poppy
the same way he'd seen through her talking about
how her job was more conducive to parenting than
his was.

Clairy didn't respond to that, though, not wanting to get into the subject any deeper.

They'd both finished eating and as Tanner took
the last drink of his beer Addie stood to gather the
remnants of their meal.

When he saw that, he did the same.

"What happens now?" he inquired as he did. "Tonight? Tomorrow? I know people talk about babies
keeping them up all night…"

"Poppy needs a middle-of-the-night feeding still.
Do you know anything about giving a baby a bottle?"

"I do not. In fact I've never so much as held a
baby," he informed her.

"Never?"

"I wasn't raised to be that kind of guy…" he said,
making Addie wonder what that meant.

But it was getting late, so she didn't ask. "Well,
I don't want to teach you at two or three in the

morning, so I guess you can have one more night's sleep—although there will be crying, so—"

"Hers or yours?"

A joke.

And it surprised Addie because it seemed so unlike him and she smiled in spite of herself.

"Poppy's," she answered. "I'm just the zombie who'll be shuffling around here to get her to stop."

"Is there anything I *can* do?"

Why did she like that he offered that?

"No, you'd probably just get in the way and make it take longer." And she didn't relish the idea of seeing how he looked straight from bed or finding out when she was half-asleep what kind of impact that might have on her.

"And tomorrow?" Tanner asked as he discarded his empty beer bottle.

Addie didn't want to answer that.

So she stalled by putting her water glass in the dishwasher, turning off all but the light over the sink and saying, "I leave this on so I can see when I come downstairs to get Poppy's bottle."

He nodded but didn't let go of what she knew was coming. "We need to have the DNA tests done so we can get that underway," he reminded.

"I suppose you want me to make an appointment?"

"Actually," he told her, "I called the hospital after I left Gloria's this afternoon… They said we could come into the lab there without an appointment."

Everything was becoming too real for Addie and she couldn't force herself to dive in.

"So how about we do that early?" he suggested. "Then I'll get to work on the bathroom? Or is there something else you want me to do?"

"You better do the bathroom," she said in a voice as loud as she could muster,

Feeling as if she just needed to escape, she started to walk around him to do that.

He stopped her with a big hand clasped around her upper arm and a soft "Hey…"

Addie looked up into that face, those eyes, and found him frowning slightly down at her.

"I mean it—I'm not looking to hurt you," he repeated.

"But you will if you take Poppy away from me," she heard herself say, every bit of the vulnerability and fear she felt in her voice.

"Come on…" he nearly whispered, begging her to understand.

And she did. As much as she could. It just didn't help.

"We're both in a tough position here," he said, his hand tightening around her arm just enough to make her all the more aware of it. Of the warmth, the strength of that calloused palm gently holding her bare arm…

Of feeling so good despite everything…

"When my mother was involved…" he said then, sounding as if what he was saying was difficult for him, "…things with Della and me…they weren't

done the way they should have been. I was a kid...
I didn't know which way was up. And my mother...
she was a bear cat..." He shook his head. "This time
it has to be done right. You see that, don't you?"

"There's only so much I can see beyond what it
means to me, to Poppy..." she said, the tears flooding her eyes again too fast for her to keep them at
bay this time.

"She could be my blood, Addie. *My* family..."

"She *is* my blood, my family..."

"But not quite as close..."

That only made it worse and Addie felt her bottom lip quiver even as she continued to struggle to
keep from crying.

Tanner looked into her eyes with those so, so blue
ones of his filled with what looked like an agony of
his own. His thumb stroked her arm to comfort her,
making her even more aware of his touch...

And liking it even better...

"Let's just both try to trust that this will work out
the way it's meant to, huh?" he implored.

Addie raised her chin as her only concession to
that, drowning a little in his eyes holding hers as
surely as his hand held her arm.

And for some completely uncalled-for, impossible-
to-understand reason, what popped into her mind at
that moment was the thought of him pulling her up
against that body that was a wall of masculinity, and
holding her...

Comforting her...

Kissing her...

It made no sense.

Helpless to figure out anything and knowing she needed to get away from him before she did or said anything more, she shrugged and whispered a simple "See you in the morning."

For a moment he kept his hand on her arm, kept her there, continuing to study her face.

Then he let go of her and she wasted no time getting away from him and whatever it was that caused her to still be thinking about having those arms of his wrapped around her.

Chapter Four

"Congratulations on the bakery, Lexie," Tanner said to his soon-to-be sister-in-law.

It was not quite ten o'clock on Monday morning when Tanner arrived at his brother Micah's brewery.

"I'm so excited!" Lexie said enthusiastically after thanking him.

"But she has an appointment at the bank to sign the papers, so she has to get going," Micah said pointedly and more to her than to Tanner.

"Don't let me keep you," Tanner encouraged, to send her on her way.

Micah and Lexie Parker had been childhood friends, but behind that friendship Micah had had a huge crush on Lexie. It had been a rocky road for them to get together, but now they were engaged and

Lexie had just made a deal to buy the local bakery. It seemed as if everything had worked out for them, and Tanner was happy for his brother.

After exchanging goodbyes, Lexie gave Micah a quick kiss, and left them to go from the barn that housed the brewery into the back door of the house where she'd grown up.

"Pops said you were coming by this morning," Micah said after watching her leave. "You need a case of the beer you like?"

"You said you'd keep me in beer as long as I'm here," Tanner reminded. "I'm holding you to it."

"I'll throw in a few bottles of the citrus-flavored one that we just bottled for the first time so you can tell me what you think."

"Great," Tanner said as he followed his brother into the heart of the brewery.

"You moved into the old Markham place yesterday?" Micah asked along the way.

"I did."

"How're things going?"

"To be honest I don't really know how to answer that," Tanner said, thinking about how the evening before had ended, about the tension between him and Addie.

And about her eyes full of tears that she'd fought off. Tears he'd put there and felt rotten for. Thinking about how, for what had to be some really screwed-up reason, he'd had the urge to pull her into his arms to try to ease the fears he was causing. At least he *thought* it was that because that was the only thing that made sense. It couldn't have been more than that. Even if it might have felt—just a little—like more than that...

"You've been with the baby now, right?" Micah said. "Did you feel some kind of instant, instinctive bond that made you know you're the father? Did you see Mom or Dad or Big Ben or us in her? Does she have our color eyes, something like that?"

"No. To all of it. Except that yeah, I've seen her—sort of from a distance—"

"From a distance?"

"Addie was holding her and I just kind of looked over at her."

"That's it? You didn't get any closer? You haven't held her or anything? I thought that was why you moved in over there—to get the hang of it."

"Yeah, it is. I just... When push came to shove..." Tanner shook his head in discomfort. "I've never been afraid of anything like I am of that kid."

Micah laughed. "Don't say that to anyone else—you'll put a stain on how tough we marines are."

"No kidding, man. I've had an insurgent's knife at my throat that didn't shake me up like this does. I think I'm still in shock or something... What the hell am I going to do if she's mine?"

"First things first," Micah repeated what Tanner had said when Tanner had initially told Micah and their grandfather what was going on. "Find out if she *is* yours."

"Yeah, I was up this morning before Addie or the baby, decided there was too much to do to wait around, so I left a note that I'd go over to the hospital lab and have my test, and Addie could take the baby when she was ready. I did that on my way over here. The lab said it would take four to five days for results. I pleaded with them to put a rush on it. They said they would try but I'm not sure that meant anything but that they wanted to shut me up and get me out of there."

He'd persuaded himself that going in ahead of Addie today was the best use of time all the way around. But he *could* have started some of the work on the bathroom and gone later, with Addie. He *could* have stuck around long enough for what he was there to do—learn how to take care of the baby.

But he hadn't. He'd had a wave of anxiety this morning thinking about this, about what he was going to do if he proved to be Poppy's father, how he could manage, if he could manage… and he'd needed some air, some space, to calm down.

"And how is it with Addie?" Micah asked.

"Do you want to tell me to be nice and not to try to score with her, too?" Tanner asked facetiously, wondering if his brother was as admiring and protective of Addie as their grandfather had proven to be.

"*Are* you thinking about trying to score with her?" Micah said with surprise.

"No," Tanner scoffed because that was true. Despite that strange inclination he'd had the night before.

Accepting that, Micah said, "I just meant is she friendly toward you or are the two of you at odds?"

"She's a little prickly," he answered, opting for the word she'd used without complaining because the truth was her touchiness kept him alert for the possibility that she might be as mercurial and high-strung as her sister had been. "But what Big Ben said is true—she's had a rough time for a while with the family stuff and then to get left at the altar, too? That's a lot. Then I show up and…this isn't easy for her. She loves that baby. She's scared I'm gonna take her away…" And he'd meant it when he'd said he didn't want to hurt her, but he could see where there might not be a way around it. If Poppy was his daughter, his family, he couldn't just ignore that because becoming a father hadn't been in his game plan and he might not know exactly what to do to take care of her yet.

"So living under the same roof with Addie…" Micah said, "…how miserable is that going to be?"

Really miserable, he hoped. More miserable than it had been so far.

Because if it got more miserable maybe that would keep him from feeling what he'd felt last night when his hand was around her arm and he'd become more aware than he'd wanted to be of how soft and warm her skin was.

Maybe a slightly healthier dose of misery would keep him from thinking about the fine, delicate lines of her features, and about how he'd realized, when he'd looked down into it from a close vantage point, that she had as perfect a face as he'd ever seen.

Maybe more misery would keep him from thinking about how her hair was as shiny as silk, or picturing brown eyes that were luminous even without tears in them, and or lips that were hard to look at without wanting to kiss.

"It's probably better that we don't get too comfortable," he said in response to his brother's question. "Seems like that could just make the end of this worse."

"So you'll keep your guard up," his brother concluded.

"Oh yeah," Tanner said instantly and emphatically. Because that was what he fully intended to do.

And he'd ramp up his marine training full force to accomplish it.

Telling herself that she had no choice, once Poppy was up, fed and dressed, Addie took her to the lab at the hospital to have her DNA sample taken. She hadn't been happy to read Tanner's note that he'd gone in for his test without them, but maybe that was for the best. Though the ordeal had been physically painless for Poppy, it had been emotionally wrenching for Addie.

Afterward, she'd taken Poppy to Kelly's so she could get more work done around the house. When Kelly asked her if she was all right, Addie had claimed she was. But she found she couldn't talk about her feelings, not even with her best friend.

Instead she kissed Poppy, left her with Kelly and returned to the house, crying in her car most of the drive home, managing to curb it only when her adoption attorney finally returned the call she'd placed to him so she could have her legal questions answered.

Tanner's truck was outside when she did get home. After making sure there were no outward signs that the morning had affected her, she went inside.

He'd started working on the bathroom, and beyond announcing she was there, Addie said nothing and got to her own work for the day to escape all that was going through her mind—getting rid of the ancient carpeting in the living room.

She'd gotten instructions on how to do that from the local flooring contractor, who had advised her to vacuum it first, to remove as much as possible of the dust that had accumulated on it over the years. She'd done that before moving in so that Poppy wouldn't be breathing in any of it.

Today's job was much bigger. The flooring contractor had explained that she would first need to cut the carpet into manageable portions to roll and remove. After that she'd pry up the tack strips, pull off the multitude of staples and remove the rest of the padding.

Unfortunately, the tedium of the job didn't occupy her mind as much as she'd hoped. As she proceeded to cut up the carpet, she was unable to keep her mental wheels from rolling.

She'd been a wreck after Della died, but after grieving for her dad, then her mom, she'd known what to expect. She'd known that at first every day was a bad day, then here and there she would have a not-so-bad day before an actual good day would happen, and that, eventually, the good days took over.

Having Poppy in her life, having Poppy to care for, had helped her get to the mostly-good-days phase before Tanner had shown up. But his being here had made her grief rise to the surface all over again.

Tanner's presence had brought too many things to the fore and it was causing her to be more emotional than she wanted to be. Especially at a time when she knew she needed her wits about her.

So, as she worked on the floors, she told herself it all just had to stop. She had to settle down before she made anything with Tanner worse. She had to think straight and be unemotional. And she certainly couldn't be ogling or turning to mush over the very man who had caused Della pain and could now rob Addie of the chance to raise Poppy.

She had to toughen up.

She knew that she had to present a strong front, not a weak, weepy one, because she was up against a cool, calm and calculated marine. Normally, she considered herself a strong woman, but she'd just had a lot thrown at her lately.

A lot that she'd handled, she reminded herself. That she'd gotten through. Just the way she would this.

Of course it didn't help matters that this was coming when she was also still contending with being dumped.

But regardless, the last thing she would let happen was to let Tanner's looks and sex appeal get to her. Or suck her into anything that could lead her to more misery.

On top of everything else she couldn't lose sight of the way he'd been with Della. She couldn't forgive him for it. And she had to protect herself from any chance that those looks and that sex appeal might wear her down.

She was going to be like that floor, she decided when she'd finally rid it of all the remnants of the carpeting. The wood had clearly been through some hard times, but beyond a few scratches, some loss of its luster, it was still there, still resilient.

And so was she.

"I think the first thing you should probably do is stop acting like she might give you cooties if you get too close, and hold her," Addie advised Tanner when she returned home from picking the baby up at Kelly's.

While Addie was gone, Tanner had finished his work on the bathroom. He'd showered, shaved and changed into another pair of camo pants and one of the T-shirts that made his attributes hard to overlook—khaki-colored this time. And yes, he again smelled of that heady, fresh ocean air cologne. But Addie was ignoring it.

On her way out the door to get Poppy, she'd tested his commitment to this arrangement by suggesting that he have his first lesson in baby care when she got back.

Tanner had not seemed keen on the idea but he had agreed. So they were now outside, sitting on the porch steps. Addie had Poppy lying on her lap, the baby's head positioned at her jean-clad knees and her tiny feet at Addie's stomach.

Tanner was as far away from both of them as he could get, his back against the chipped and peeling rail post on his side.

"Does she *have* cooties?" he asked in a lame attempt at a joke.

"She does not."

"How breakable is she?"

"Well, you should always be careful with her," Addie said as if it was no joking matter, her arms forming a halo around the baby. "And there's some technique involved, but otherwise she's fairly pliable."

"No cooties and pliable..." he repeated. "Now, *that's* a recommendation." Then he tilted his head in observation and said, "How am I supposed to get this going with you hovering over her like there's falling debris?"

Oh.

Addie hadn't realized it but when he pointed it out she guessed she wasn't really giving him free access. In fact she was basically blocking him since she was protectively hunched almost completely over the baby.

She sat up straight, scooped Poppy into both hands and held her out to the man who might be her father.

He did not hold his hands out to receive her.

"I hold her like that?" he asked skeptically.

"No, let her head rest in the crook of your elbow and put your other arm under the rest of her like a sling."

"Does she still have that floppy-head thing?"

"A little. You have to give her some support but she's getting better. For now just let her head rest on your elbow," Addie reiterated.

He put his arms in the formation she'd described and she set Poppy in them.

The problem was that he'd made the formation fairly far from his body, and once Addie had handed Poppy over, he didn't pull her in any closer.

"It helps if you hold her against you." And even as Addie gave that recommendation she tried not to think about being up against that body herself…

A slight, sort-of grimace went across Tanner's face but he stiffly brought his arms in, not actually looking down at the infant even once she was there.

"Poppy, this is Tanner. Tanner, this is Poppy," Addie kiddingly introduced them, hoping that might prompt him to actually take a look at the baby.

He got the hint and—still rigidly—peered down at the chubby-cheeked little darling with her soft feathers of brown hair, her Cupid's bow mouth, and her big eyes checking him out.

"Hi?" he said as if he'd just been introduced to a suspicious stranger.

Addie couldn't help laughing at that. "She probably won't answer you."

Tanner's gaze returned to Addie. "I've heard you talking to her," he countered.

"She doesn't answer me, either."

That made his lips twitch with a faint smile before he said, "Now what do I do with her?"

"Relax?" Addie suggested. Although despite the fact that he was stiff, there was still something much too appealing, much too sexy, in the sight of that tiny bundle against his broad chest, his muscular arms cradling her, his big hands so cautiously holding her…

"I think relaxing might not be in the cards yet," he muttered into Addie's wandering thoughts. "Can we just get on with it?"

Just getting on with it seemed like a good idea…

As the remainder of the afternoon and the evening passed and it grew close to Poppy's bedtime, Tanner never did relax. Or do anything with Poppy very well.

Addie showed him every which way to hold a baby and he was no more skillful with one way than with another. Even when they moved into the kitchen so Addie could heat the shepherd's pie Kelly had sent for their dinner—when Addie only furtively kept an eye on Tanner, thinking that not being watched might make him loosen up—he was still stiff as a board.

While showing him how to change a wet diaper he stood so far from the changing table that she couldn't imagine that he'd learned anything.

Which he hadn't, because later, when there was a dirty diaper to change, she'd had to return to step one. And he'd made it clear that he didn't relish the chore no matter what.

With close supervision, she had him first give Poppy her late-afternoon bottle and then the before-bed bottle, and he was no better with the second round of that, either.

Things were going so poorly with the lessons that, for Poppy's sake and because the infant had become increasingly fussy, Addie decided against the bath she'd planned.

Addie also took over burping Poppy after the bedtime bottle. The marine was so ineffective at it in any position that she didn't want to risk putting Poppy down to sleep with a gas bubble that might give her a stomachache.

The final instruction was to turn on the nightlight and monitor, and how to position Poppy in her crib for a safe slumber.

By then everything had gone so poorly that Addie wouldn't have been surprised if Tanner left the nursery, went down the stairs and out the front door, never to be seen again.

Instead he stepped away from the crib and said,

"I want to see if I can tell why that outlet in the kitchen isn't working," and fled downstairs.

After he was gone, Addie whispered to the baby, "I'm sorry, sweetheart, but it's good that he did so badly because we need to scare him away. Work up some smelly poos tomorrow—it can only help."

Then she kissed Poppy good-night and told her to sleep tight before going in search of Tanner.

She didn't find him in the kitchen, though his toolbox was on the floor near the dead outlet. But he'd done some work apparently, because the cover plate was off.

Looking through the window over the kitchen sink, Addie saw the outside light was on, illuminating the backyard. She went out back to look for Tanner.

Sure enough, he was hunkered down near a hole in the wooden siding, approximately where the outlet was on the inside.

"What's going on?" she asked as she went over to him.

"I could be wrong but I'm thinking you may have had a visit from a squirrel or a mouse," Tanner answered. "They can get into the wall and chew through the wires."

"Wouldn't that electrocute them?"

"Yep, that's what it would do."

"So there could be a dead squirrel or a dead mouse in there?"

"Or even a rat. It's possible," he confirmed.

"Oh, yuck... I've been trying to get to the bottom

of a smell that I can't get rid of. Could it be coming from a dead thing?" she asked with disgust.

"Could be. The hole is too small for me to see much even with the flashlight, though, and I can't get my hand into it, either. Why don't you see if yours will fit, feel around?"

"*Feel around* in the wall for a *dead* thing?" Addie exclaimed.

"My hand won't fit," he reiterated.

"Uh-uh, helping with the house is your part of our deal," Addie insisted, glad she had an out.

"But my hand won't fit," he said again. "Nothing'll hurt you—I've turned off the power to the outlet and dead things don't bite."

It won't hurt you...

She doesn't bite...

Those were very similar things she'd said to him in the course of telling him what to do with Poppy when he'd shown some hesitancy and distaste. Was there some message he was sending with this?

Or maybe she was just imagining it...

"You can use one of those rubber gloves from under the bathroom sink," he was saying. "Just reach inside, feel around. If you find something, grab hold of whatever you can—the body, the tail, the head, whatever. Just don't squeeze or pull too hard, we don't know how decomposed it might be. Then ease it out—carefully, gently."

More than once with Poppy she'd cautioned him to be careful, to be gentle.

Was this some kind of retaliation?

But what would he be retaliating for? She'd merely done what she'd agreed to do—she'd begun to teach him how to care for a baby. It wasn't her fault if he was bad at it.

Still, something about this seemed off to her...

"Is this a joke?"

"A dead animal in your wall and frayed wires are no joke. And if you're gonna be a homeowner, things are going to happen that you'll need to take care of," he said simply, just the way she'd informed him that when it came to kids, there would be bigger messes than a dirty diaper—like spontaneous vomiting in the car seat or in a movie theater.

Then he said, "It'll smell worse once it's out in the open. If you can't take it you can hold your breath..."

That was almost exactly what she'd said when he'd balked at Poppy's dirty diaper.

"Okay, what's really going on with the outlet?" Addie demanded, thinking she was calling his bluff.

"Come over here, take a whiff. Tell me if I'm wrong."

She did, moving close to where he was squatted, bending over to put her face near the hole and breathing deeply.

Not even his cologne helped. It was definitely the odor she'd been chasing, only much stronger.

Recoiling, she jolted upright and took a step back. "I can't put my hand in there," she admitted, regardless of whatever ulterior motive he might have with this little game.

Her admission seemed to give him some satisfaction as he sat back on his heels, his hands on his knees, peering up at her. "Okay… Then I'll make another deal with you," he said. "I'll take care of this if you quit what you're doing with Poppy."

"What am I doing?" she asked innocently.

"Pouring it on thick," he said. "Not giving me a chance to get any good at one thing before you pile on a dozen more. All the scare tactics—"

"I'm just telling it like it is."

"You ran me through ways to hold her in rapid fire. You changed that first diaper as if you were in a race so I couldn't really learn how to do it. You gave me a hard time every chance you got. You told me horror stories about car seats and swimming pools and unlocked cupboards and gummy vitamins. You even gave me guff about how I'll never be able to handle anything if I can't even get a burp out of her now—what does puberty have to do with that?"

Okay, so maybe she *had* poured it on a little thick.

But she still wasn't admitting anything.

"You *said* you want to be prepared…"

"I don't need to be hearing *now* about how I might trip on the train of her wedding dress and bring her down with me when I walk her down the aisle."

Even the thought of Poppy's wedding stabbed Addie, because if it came to Tanner walking Poppy down the aisle Addie knew that she would likely be history—the aunt who hadn't been involved in Poppy's life after her father had packed her up and taken her with him to wherever in the world he went…

Tanner got to his feet, standing tall and straight in front of her again. "Give me a break while I try to get used to doing what's as foreign to me as taking a dead thing out of a wall is to you," he said.

"As if touching a dead thing *isn't* foreign to you?"

He scoffed at that. "I'm one of four brothers who grew up on a farm—poking dead things, daring each other to touch them, to pick them up, was part of that. While you did what? Played with dolls when you were really young, then babysat when you were a teenager, right?"

Not wrong.

But in spite of that she said, "That's sexist. I knew boys who babysat."

"But what did you do?" he demanded. "Babysit or mess with dead things?"

"I didn't mess with dead things," was all she would say.

"The point is, you have your skills and I have mine."

"Yours being dead things?"

"Among others. I'm not squeamish about this. But babies are not in my wheelhouse. Right now. If you want me to do this, stop piling it on with the baby stuff and give me the chance to ease into it. To get at least a *little* competent at one thing before you expect me to move on and learn how to do another."

He still wasn't going to be good at it, she told

herself, holding onto that hope as well as the hope that once he did learn what it took he'd want out.

"I'll try to be more patient and go slower," she promised, knowing she'd have to, because he'd seen through her tactics. And because she needed *not* to contend with a dead thing in her wall.

For a moment his blue eyes bored into her, letting her know he expected her to keep her word. Then he said, "I'll get whatever is in there out but if you go back to what you did today, so help me, I'll dig it out of the trash and put it back."

Addie took a deep, resigned breath and sighed. "Just take it out."

He arched one eyebrow at her to let her know he meant the threat, before he said, "I'll have to cut into the drywall inside."

Something else occurred to her with that.

"So it's a pretty good guess from the smell that something got in there and chewed the wires. The only way you'll be able to *get* to the wires is to cut the drywall inside, isn't it? You've known all along that you didn't need a smaller hand to reach into that hole from out here," she accused.

Tanner smiled and somehow the crinkles his smile put at the corners of his eyes only made him more handsome even as it confirmed that she'd seen through him, too.

"Maybe," he answered, like her, not admitting more than he had to. "If you'd reached up there and there wasn't an animal I might have been able to just change out the receptacle."

"Bull! One whiff and you knew there was something dead in there, Mr. Master-Of-Dead-Things."

His smile turned into a grin. "Maybe," he repeated.

Clairy's own anxiety rose up again at the thought that he was ensuring she made good on her part of their agreement to teach him how to care for Poppy. But the better the lessons, the more proficient she knew he would become and the more likely it was that he could take Poppy away. And suddenly Addie had to address her own fears with him, she had to put her worries out on the table with him.

"Will you really do it if you're Poppy's biological father? Will you pack her up and disappear with her to raise her yourself, and that'll be it for me being in her life?"

The humor and satisfaction he'd found in making his point evaporated. "Oh, Addie…" he said softly, compassionately.

"Will you?" she demanded.

His eyebrows arched in an expression of confusion, indecision, frustration. "Please understand… I'm just wrapping my head around the chance that Poppy might be my flesh and blood. I haven't had enough time here or with her for me to feel much besides… stunned. The whole time with Poppy today I kept wondering if I'm supposed to have instant feelings… does it mean she's not mine if that hasn't happened yet… And I'm a little afraid of even letting it happen because what if I do start to accept that she's mine, what if I do start loving her, and then find out she isn't mine…"

Addie was surprised at his honesty, at how many things were torturing him, at how much was on his mind that he'd been stoically keeping under wraps.

And since he was being honest with her, she had to be honest with herself. She realized that she had her own mixed feelings about him gaining any sense of attachment to Poppy—that for her own sake she didn't want him to, and that maybe today she'd run interference, trying to keep them from bonding. But she also realized that, for Poppy's sake—if he was Poppy's dad—she didn't want him to lack feelings or attachment to Poppy so she was doing Poppy a disservice if she stood in the way of that…

Tanner sighed. "I'll tell you this," he said as if it were a recent realization of his own, "It wasn't easy not having my own dad as I was growing up. If Poppy is mine, I'm gonna be her dad. I'm gonna do everything to be the dad I didn't get to have. Do I have a game plan for how the hell I'm going to do that? No. There's so much I'll have to figure out, so many logistics I'll have to work with… it won't be easy… But I do know… I *have* decided… that I'll do whatever needs to be done—"

"Even if it means I just become her distant forgotten aunt…" Addie whispered to herself in abject misery.

That seemed to give him pause, to bring her and her feelings back into the picture for him again.

Then, as if he'd reached a new element in beginning to consider how the future might actually play out for them both, he said, "I won't let that happen. I'll make sure she still knows you. I'll make sure you're always a part of her life. I'll make sure that we work out something so she spends time with you, so she comes to visit, so you can come to wherever we might be to see her."

Addie knew that in that moment he meant what he was saying. And that that was something. It was just so, so much less than she wanted. And it was only hypothetical so what were the odds that it would ultimately happen?

"I guess that's something…" she said, her heart breaking because even though she'd sworn that she would fight for Poppy, she knew from talking to her adoption lawyer today that if a biological father appeared on the scene and wanted custody, the court would be inclined to grant it. That even with Tanner being in the military, if he presented the desire to raise Poppy, the means and method for caring for her, and without any indications that he was unfit, it was highly unlikely for an aunt to be granted custody over Poppy's own father.

"I guess I should be grateful that you won't cut me out completely…" she muttered.

"I'll make sure it's better than that," he said as if he was committed to it.

But even good intentions could go by the wayside and she didn't have much hope that fighting for visitation as nothing more than an aunt would get her further than those good intentions.

But with everything hanging in the balance until the DNA results, there wasn't much use arguing it.

"Come on," he said then, clearly trying for a lighter tone. "Let's get this dead thing out of your wall."

He didn't move though, he waited for her to lead the way, apparently unsure if she was going to allow them to move on from this for now.

Addie took a breath, swallowed back her own emotions and went back into the house.

Then, telling herself that she not only needed not to alienate the man who could hold her future relationship with Poppy in his hands, but that even his proving-his-point charade had been more enjoyable than what she'd just induced, she tried for a lighter tone, too.

"I think maybe your mother *should* have made you babysit instead of letting you mess around with dead things."

As he opened the toolbox on the floor in front of the exposed outlet he said, "*My* mother? She probably would have grounded me if I'd said I was going to babysit. Unless I'd had a masterplan to corner the market and hire other people to do it so I could become a babysitting mogul."

"Rather than learn a skill you could use in life? A skill you didn't end up with and now might need?"

"Taking care of kids or babies was not a skill my mother cared about us having. Childcare experts was nowhere on the list of what her sons had to be."

"What did her sons have to be?"

"Tough. Fearless. Aggressive. Determined. Driven. Ambitious. Hell-bent."

"That's a long list of extremes," Addie observed.

"That was Mom," he confirmed matter-of-factly.

He'd taken a small saw out of the toolbox and now proceeded to cut through the drywall.

Addie leaned a hip against the edge of the nearest countertop and watched, noting what seemed impossible *not* to notice—his massive hand gripping the saw and the flexing of the muscles in his forearm and biceps.

When he paused to flash some light into the hole he'd made—she assumed to see how much more he had to cut away—she restarted the conversation. "What about having sensitive sons?"

Tanner chuckled at that. "*Sensitive* sons?" he repeated. "No, that was not anywhere on the program."

He took up the saw for a second time and went to work removing more of the wall, again making too much noise for either of them to speak.

Merritt was a small town, so of course Addie had known who Raina Camden was. She'd also known that the woman was rigid, stern and standoffish. Mrs. Camden wasn't very well liked, or thought to be warm or friendly even among the other women in town. In fact, frequently Addie had heard it said that Raina Camden thought she was better than everyone else. And certainly, having witnessed Raina in action seventeen years ago, when confronted with the issue between Tanner and Della, Addie knew firsthand that the woman had been fierce and formidable.

But Addie had no idea how Mrs. Camden had raised her sons.

When Tanner stopped sawing and pulled away another piece of drywall, the rank smell flooded the kitchen.

She drew back but it didn't seem to faze Tanner, who said, "You have a dead squirrel all right. Get a trash bag and hold it open."

As he took a work glove out of the toolbox and reached into the opening in the wall, Addie hurried for a black plastic trash bag. Opening it, she kept her arms stretched as far out as possible to await the disposal, breathing only shallowly. And not wanting a clear view, she also turned her head so she had only a peripheral view while Tanner pulled the dead squirrel out by the tail and dropped it into the bag.

"Gross..." Addie judged with a shiver of revulsion.

Tanner merely removed the work glove and let it fall into the trash, too, before taking the bag from her and cinching it shut.

"I'll get rid of this."

"I'll open the windows so we can get some fresh air in here," Addie said. "Can I spray air freshener into the hole in the wall?"

"I wouldn't bother with any perfumey stuff. It probably brought in fleas and who knows how long it was in there decomposing and leaving other souvenirs. I'd go with bleach," he recommended on his way out the back door.

Addie ran to fling open windows and then liberally sprayed a bleach solution she'd been using elsewhere in the old house.

She was still at it when Tanner came in to wash his hands in the laundry room washbasin.

Then he returned to the outlet, shining his flashlight into the opening he'd made. "Yep, chewed wires."

"Can you fix that? And the wall?" Addie asked.

"I can," he said, this time being straightforward.

Craning to peer higher up into the hole, he said, "Looks like he got in, did the damage to this one spot and got zapped for it before he could do worse. I should be able to wrap the wires, patch the drywall, then seal up where he got in outside. For tonight I'll just get this mess—and what he left inside the wall—cleaned up."

Tanner reached into his toolbox for another work glove and put it on.

Addie was trying to keep her mind off the stench that seemed to mingle with the bleach rather than be nullified by it, and started to think about what he'd said about his mother. Which reminded her yet again of Raina Camden's response to what had happened seventeen years ago.

"Did your mother not want grandchildren?" she asked as he went into the bathroom and returned with a scrap of cardboard.

"Couldn't say," he answered, kneeling in front of

the hole again. "The only time it ever came up was with Della and me."

"And what your mother wanted was for you to become a marine," Addie said, basing the conclusion on the determination Raina Camden had displayed that her son was going to Annapolis and nothing and nobody was going to stop him.

Tanner laughed slightly again. "Actually Mom wasn't thrilled with any of us joining the military," he informed her as he reached inside the wall to pull out chunks of the drywall that had fallen away during the sawing phase. "But it was what we all wanted to do—our father was in the military and we all wanted to follow his lead. I think it was maybe a way to feel connected to him, to *having* a father…"

Tanner paused a moment, then said, "Anyway, Micah had fought the going-into-the-military battle with Mom and won it for us all the year before that."

"What would she rather have you all do?"

"Become H.J. Camden," he answered flatly.

"The Camden Superstores guy?" Addie said when she brought the plastic-bag-lined-trash basket from under the sink and set it beside him so he could dispose of what he was pulling out. "I remember Della saying something about a connection between those Camdens and you."

"H.J. and my great-grandfather Hector were brothers—H.J. and Hector Camden."

"But your mom didn't want you to be like your own great-grandfather? She wanted you to be like the other guy?"

"Oh, yeah. H.J. and his son and his grandsons."

"That seems strange."

"H.J. and Hector were close but not alike," Tanner explained, now taking a paintbrush from the toolbox and using it and the cardboard scrap like a broom and dustpan on the floor of the inside of the wall.

"Hector—my great-grandfather—was a laid-back, easygoing guy who just wanted to be a small farmer. Who was *content*—a dirty word to my mother—to be a small farmer. Same with my grandfather to this day. Sort of the same with my dad, although not with farming—according to what we've been told, when he had to take a medical discharge from the air force for an issue with his knee, he still wanted to fly. As long as he could be a pilot, he didn't care who owned the plane."

"And in your mother's eyes not owning his own plane made him not…ambitious enough?" Addie guessed. "Did your mother *not* want you all to just be happy doing whatever you wanted to do?"

"She wanted us to be succeed-at-all-costs guys like the other Camdens. She loved my great-grandfather, my grandfather, my dad, but she thought they were…" Tanner made a face and said quietly, "…kind of patsies."

"Oh…" Addie said, hearing in his voice that it was not something Tanner wanted to admit.

"Yeah… For starters, Mom had a grudge against the other side of the family. There's a story that the Camden Superstores idea was a suggestion Hector made to H.J., so she was convinced that if Hector hadn't been such a pushover, we would have owned half of it all—something neither Hector nor my grandfather ever agreed with. And then, when my dad died piloting the plane that also killed H.J.'s son, grandsons and granddaughters-in-law—"

"A private plane?"

"The other Camdens' private jet, yeah. There was a family vacation planned for H.J. his son and his son's wife—everyone calls her GiGi—"

"She's still alive?"

"H.J. hurt his back right before the trip, couldn't go, so his daughter-in-law stayed home with him to take care of him while his son, his grandsons and their wives went ahead and went. It saved H.J. and GiGi, who ended up raising the ten kids left behind, H.J.'s great-grandchildren, GiGi's grandchildren. They're our cousins, all close to our ages."

"I would have thought your dad would have flown for a commercial airline," Addie said.

"No, after he left the air force he became the pilot for the other Camdens' so he could have better hours than he would have had as a commercial pilot but in order to keep flying."

"And the crash?"

"It was caused by a mechanical problem. But Mom had resented Dad becoming a worker bee for the other Camdens anyway, and that resentment grew over losing my dad because of it. His death cemented her grudge against them."

Whether or not the grudge over the stores was warranted, Addie could understand Raina Camden's bitterness at losing her husband. But she wasn't sure how that related to the way she'd raised her kids.

"Did your mother want to raise sons who would dish out some kind of payback?" she said.

Tanner shook his head. "She just *didn't* want us to be like Hector and my grandfather—or even like my dad, because even though she thought the air force had toughened him up, she didn't like that he was willing to be a Camden employee rather than going out to make a big splash himself and build his own dynasty. She said she tried to push him into that before we lost him but it just wasn't who he was— he was too mellow. That left us—Micah—who was two years old, and Quinn, Dalton and me who were barely a year. And she decided she was damn sure going to make her sons as driven as H.J.'s side of the family so we didn't end up being walked all over— that was a big thing to her."

"Was there money from the other Camdens to help raise you all?"

"There was an insurance settlement."

"And what about the relationship between you guys and your cousins?"

"My mother's resentment squashed that for a long time. Ben always wanted us to have one. Eventually he convinced Mom that our visiting the other side of the family, getting to know them, might help some of the other side of the family's ambitions rub off on us, so she let us go to Denver summers, have a few other visits with them."

"So, to harden her boys, your mother was hard

on you all?" Addie said, getting back to what they were talking about before the family history.

"That's about it, yeah. She set us up to compete with each other for damn near everything—lose the competition, lose whatever it was we wanted."

"It was her goal to have you all to fight for things?"

"Yep. She figured that if she raised us to fight for what we wanted, it would mean whatever any one of us did in life was done no holds barred. Actually, that was how Micah won the first battle to join the service—she wanted us all to become big business moguls—"

"Like the other Camdens. Did she want you to compete with them or run them out of business?"

"She would have liked it if we'd set our sights on them. But basically her aim was just to make us the kind of men who never gave an inch. She said that was the way to succeed and that's what she wanted of us all."

"But Micah wanted to join the military instead?"

"We all did. Like I said, we all had this idea of following in our father's footsteps. But as the oldest, Micah reached the point of acting on it first. When he let her know that's what he wanted to do, he had to battle for it before she would even entertain the idea. Since that's what he did, she respected him and gave in to it because full-steam-ahead was more important to her than *what* we chose to do."

"And Micah's determination paved the way for the rest of you?" Addie asked.

Tanner laughed again. "Not quite, no. Nothing was ever that easy. It helped some—Micah's sticking to his guns caused her to accept the military over big business. But then she set up the hurdles for the rest of us. Higher grade point averages. Who could use the legacy left by Dad being Annapolis alumnus—because she wouldn't let more than one of us do that. Not letting more than one of us tap the same person for nominations…"

Addie had had a kid here and there in her classrooms who was driven. Sometimes it made them high achievers and good students. Sometimes, when the drive was forced on them, it hurt and frustrated them and they ended up hating whoever was pressuring them and rebelling.

The Merritt Camdens seemed to have thrived.

But when Addie thought back to what she'd seen in Tanner when Della had told him she was pregnant, Addie wasn't sure what kind of humans Raina Camden's tactics had made them.

"What about outside the house—were you supposed to just compete with each other at home or with everyone?"

"Everyone," Tanner answered, dropping more of what he'd cleaned from inside the wall into the trash. "We had to be the best. We had to do the best. And we had to leave no stone unturned to get what we went after—no opportunity ignored, no advantage unused, no weakness unexplored."

"So not only didn't your mother raise her sons to be sensitive, she kind of raised you guys to be—"

"Relentless. And to never give an inch," Tanner supplied.

Addie knew her eyes were open wide, her eyebrows were arched at the idea of sentiments like that being taught to children, but she didn't know what to say. She settled on, "To me that sounds a little like a way to create bullies..."

"My grandfather wouldn't stand for that," Tanner said without offense. "He didn't interfere with anything Mom preached but he did make sure we didn't take things too far. He was all about fair play. About being decent people, doing what was right. There was no making fun of anyone or any hazing kind of stuff. We all had friends, we just weren't the guys to run against for class president, or compete with for an after-school job—or a girl—because we weren't going to give in..."

She knew he didn't intend to scare her but the information did. Because if he proved to be Poppy's biological father, the only way she still might end up getting to raise Poppy was if he *did* give in. And despite what he'd told her tonight, she still had to hold onto some amount of hope that he might.

Then for some reason her thoughts again turned to Della and something he'd mentioned the previous evening. "So with Della... Last night you said that when your mother got involved seventeen years ago it wasn't done the way it should have been..."

Seventeen years ago, after Tanner had so reluctantly conceded that he would marry her sister, he'd told his mother about the situation, and his mother had appeared on the Markhams' doorstep in a fury.

The first order of business was proof that Della was pregnant, and Raina had demanded a medical evaluation.

If Della actually was pregnant, then Raina said bluntly that there would need to be additional proof that Tanner was the father.

Even if that was the case, Raina Camden had made it clear that marriage was absolutely not an alternative. Raina had sworn that neither Della nor a baby would alter Tanner's future.

Tanner, Raina had decreed, would relinquish parental rights. Raina herself would pay child support if need be so that Tanner could go on completely unencumbered by what Raina had been convinced was a trap on Della's part.

It had been ugly.

And since Della had ultimately collapsed into even more hysteria and admitted that she wasn't actually pregnant at all, that she'd devised the lie in an attempt to persuade Tanner to come back to her and not to leave Merritt, the whole matter had ended there. For the Camdens.

But now—especially in light of how Tanner had been raised—Addie wondered how he thought it should have been handled, and that was what she asked.

Tanner had finished cleaning behind the wall, so he stood up, tossed the scrap of cardboard, the paintbrush and the second work glove in the trash.

Then he turned to face her, leaning back against the counter's edge, crossing his arms over his chest.

"I didn't want to marry Della," he said bluntly, somberly. "I didn't want to see her anymore at all. I'd broken up with her four days before she called me to say that I *had* to come to your house because she had something to tell me. Something that I *had* to know. I told her again that we were over and there was nothing I had to know. She said if I didn't come she was going to spread word—lies—that I did drugs… She said that she would give herself bruises and say I'd hit her… She made a lot of threats…said she'd ruin me, get word to the academy, if I didn't show up…"

I have a plan… Addie remembered her sister saying back then. She hadn't known Della had threatened him with all that, but she did know that Della didn't accept no for an answer herself.

But Addie kept what she did and didn't know to herself. "So you showed up and that was when she told you she was pregnant."

He nodded. "For me, going out with your sister was always just a high school thing—"

"Della *never* thought that," Addie said, feeling the need to defend her sister.

"She *said* she did. I was always honest with her— more times than I can count I told her that as soon as we graduated I was leaving for college, that things between us would end. She said that was no problem, that she was going away to school, too. That she wanted the whole college-party experience and didn't want to be tied down, either."

Addie shook her head. "That may have been what she said but she didn't mean it." Because during that same time frame, at home, Della had been talking nonstop to Addie about the day she and Tanner would get married.

But Addie didn't doubt that misleading him was what her sister had done. Della had commonly played games like that, secure in her belief that ultimately she could still make things work out the way she wanted them to.

"Well I *did* mean it," Tanner said. "And I never wavered, I never hedged. There was no reason for her to think we wouldn't go our separate ways for college."

"Unless she could stop you by saying she was pregnant," Addie concluded.

"We'd talked about having that last summer together, but by the end of senior year... I just couldn't let it go that far..." Tanner shook his head. "I liked Della, but after a while she...wore me out."

Loyalty to her sister caused Addie not to chime in. But as much as she'd loved Della, she recognized her sister in the things he was saying. Della had been temperamental, had a tendency to blow things out of proportion, take things too far. Della's highs and lows, her over-the-top expectations and her manipulations to have those expectations met had cost her friends and relationships.

"I made it through prom," Tanner was saying.

"But it was a full-on nightmare. Halfway through, Della got it into her head that our *prom story* should be that instead of going to the after-party we should elope. I thought she was kidding but she was serious…" he said, the disbelief he must have had that night echoing in his voice even now. "When I wouldn't do it, the night went downhill from there."

Addie was reasonably sure that was an understatement.

"I knew then that I had to cut the ties. That I couldn't wait until I left town in August," he confessed quietly, carefully, as if he was fully aware that he was telling this to someone who would be sympathetic to Della.

Addie still didn't say anything, torn more than he knew between her love for her sister and her understanding of what he was saying.

"But if she really had been pregnant," Tanner continued with conviction, "I wouldn't have bailed on her. It was my grandfather's influence that won out when I said I'd marry her and it would have ultimately won out if there was genuinely a call for it—regardless of what my mother wanted."

"You would have married someone you didn't love or want to marry, someone you didn't even want to date anymore?"

"If that's what I needed to do, that's what I would have done. Which also would have meant no Annapolis, because a cadet can't be married or have kids. But if there had actually been a baby…"

Another wave of fear ran through Addie at the

thought that he would have gone to that length before, confirming for her that he wouldn't do less
than that now with Poppy. "My mother was thinking clearer than I was seventeen years ago, when
it didn't occur to me that Della might be lying," he
was saying when she tuned back into the sound of
his deep voice. "But where my mother went wrong
was in taking those shots at Della—and your parents—by saying the baby might not even be mine,
by accusing Della of sleeping around. And no, I
would not have signed away my parental rights."

That struck even more fear in Addie and in light
of that she couldn't keep herself from mounting a
defense, so she said, "Is there any part of you that
thinks marrying Della would have worked out—for
you or her or a baby?"

He didn't answer immediately. "Della and I were
kids… There'd been infatuation on my part, but that
had died out. I don't know what was going on with
Della…then or eleven and a half months ago, when
she made it seem like her life was in order and then
that next morning the teenage Della was right there
again…" Once more he paused before he said, "So
no, I can't imagine how a marriage would have
lasted. Put a kid into the mix and it doesn't take an
expert to know it wouldn't have been a good situation for that kid, either. But—"

"You still would have done it?"

"I was scared out of my mind that it was going to
come to that, but if it had, I wouldn't—I *couldn't*—

have just left her and a kid hanging the way my mother would have had it."

Which answered Addie's query about how things should have been done differently seventeen years ago.

"But everything doesn't have to be so black-and-white," she felt compelled to say. "Doing the *right* thing isn't always the *best* thing."

"What would you have had me do back then?"

Of course he didn't realize it was the future that was on her mind, when they were actually talking about the past...

And in the past, in her own romantic frame of mind and aching for her sister, she'd wanted him to marry Della. It was just that now, when she was potentially facing his strong sense of right and wrong, she was pulling for a little more selfishness on his part.

Which was strange—to be hoping he *wasn't* a good guy.

But since it *was* the past that they were talking about, she focused on that.

"Okay, yes, I can see your point," she admitted. "It was an awful mess. And yes, when I thought Della was pregnant I was hoping you'd come through for her. And maybe your mother was too over-the-top, too, but looking back..." *And looking forward now...* "There isn't ever only *one* solution to a problem."

"Maybe not. But there is usually what's right and

what's wrong," he contended steadfastly, again striking fear in Addie.

Because now there really was a baby.

A baby she loved.

And if it was his…

But being that scared wasn't good. It made her scattered. And that could defeat her all on its own, she thought.

She couldn't let that happen if there was any chance that she might convince him to be the variable in Poppy's life rather than her, to grant her custody even if she couldn't win it in court, she had to compartmentalize that fear in order to keep her wits about her. As difficult as it was, she had to box it up and put it on a high shelf.

And mentally that was what she did as Tanner said in conclusion, "It was just a good thing that Della *wasn't* pregnant."

Addie merely nodded, accepting the end to this conversation that was all too unnerving to her anyway.

"We should get this trash out before any squirrel dust or fleas or whatever it brought in with it gets in the air," she suggested, to change the subject. "Then we'd better both wash our hands like we're scrubbing for surgery before we get near Poppy again."

Tanner conceded to that by pushing off the counter's edge with his hips, and taking the plastic bag out of the trash receptacle as if he was only too willing to terminate the previous conversation.

While he was outside Addie replaced the trash

bag and then met him at the washtub in the laundry room where they did scrub their hands like surgeons. Then Addie bleached the washbasin and returned to the kitchen to spray more bleach into the hole in the wall.

When she finished with that she turned around.

Tanner didn't seem to be expecting it, because the minute she did he altered the angle of his gaze in a hurry, raising it to her face from wherever it had been before.

"Time for beer?" he suggested, maybe pretending that he hadn't been ogling her, when she was fairly sure he had been.

But the idea that there was nothing left to do except relax made Addie laugh.

"You think it's time to wind down? Because we're nowhere near that yet. I had all this done last night when you got back but I have to run the dishwasher every day to make sure there are enough clean bottles and everything that goes with them—that needs to be emptied now. Formula has to be made and bottles have to be filled so they're ready for the middle of the night and tomorrow. There's a daily load of baby laundry to make sure there's enough of all that, too. Now is when I get it out of the dryer, fold it and put it in the nursery, because there's always the possibility that when Poppy wakes up to be fed during the night her pajamas will be wet or dirty. That means a change of clothes and—if it's gone through to the crib sheet, a change of that, too."

"In the middle of the night?"

"She can't be put back to bed on a wet sheet."

"You're not just saying that to make it sound worse than it really is?" he tested.

"I guess you'll see…"

Leaving it at that, Addie did the chores she'd mentioned, giving Tanner instructions at a pace he could actually learn from.

Before emptying the dishwasher she showed him how to rinse baby bottles using the one she'd fed Poppy before putting her down for the night. Then Addie opened the dishwasher door to put away the clean dishes, informing him where in the cupboards everything went.

She instructed him in how to make the formula and fill the bottles—losing one when he accidentally knocked it over before they'd put the nipple and travel cover on it.

She demonstrated where in the refrigerator the bottles were kept and lectured him about not using leftover formula and how many times a bottle could safely be reheated if—as she sometimes did—Poppy became disinterested midbottle, then hungry again half an hour later.

"How do you know she's hungry again half an hour later?" he asked, sounding genuinely interested. Damn him…

"She'll cry—"

"Why would I think she was hungry, though, if she just ate?"

"There's a hungry cry that's different than the

tired or fussy or something-hurts cries—you just need to learn and pick up on it."

Addie went on to warn him that feeding time wasn't always as efficient as what he'd seen today that sometimes it took much longer.

Once the kitchen chores were finished she led the way into the laundry room where she also outlined for him what each article of clothing was and when it was used.

The whole time they were at that she was trying hard to think of herself only as the teacher and Tanner strictly as her student. But she lapsed a little when she began to notice how the clothes all looked in his big, powerful hands that were surprisingly adept with the tiny things. Adept enough to have caught her arm last night to keep her from leaving the room... And that was all it took for her to flash back to the way it had felt—all warm, gentle strength...

"So that's it," she said, pulling herself out of the memory that was accompanied by something that almost seemed like a longing to feel it again.

She tamped down on that feeling as she placed the folded baby things into a laundry basket.

Then, wanting to get into a bigger room that would allow for more space between them, she picked up the basket and took it out to the kitchen table.

"*Now* you can start thinking about your wind-down beer," she announced as he trailed behind her, sounding cheerier than she'd intended in her efforts to hide her unwanted thoughts and feelings.

Tanner glanced at the old schoolhouse clock on the wall. "Over an hour—that's how long this took... And this is every night?"

"Unless I have the bottles and enough clean clothes and blankets and sheets to get through to the start of the next morning. But then it still has to be done in the morning so it puts a late start on whatever has to be done that day—like going to work."

His eyebrows arched at that revelation, and when he didn't say anything she hoped he was noting what that would mean to him as part of his everyday life.

If he was, he didn't let on, though. Apparently having lost his desire for a beer because he didn't go to the fridge to get one, he said, "And what about the middle-of-the-night thing?"

Addie went from the kitchen table to a cupboard drawer next to the refrigerator and took out a second receiver for the camera in the nursery.

"The third-grade teacher at my school gave me her baby monitor because she didn't need it anymore and it saved me the expense of a newer one. It came with two of these because it's kind of outdated and there isn't an app to just put on our phones. So here's your monitor. You'll be able to see the crib and hear Poppy cry."

"I heard everything last night. I stayed in bed because I didn't want to get in the way."

"Still, you should have this, especially being downstairs. Taking care of a baby means you need to know what's going on with her all the time, no matter what you're doing or where you are in the house."

Tanner joined her at the counter, leaning one hip against it so she could teach him how to use the receiver and so he could see what the screen showed of the nursery.

"So if you're in there I'll see you, too," he said for no reason Addie could fathom.

"Only if I'm at the crib. The point is to hear Poppy and to be able to keep an eye on her."

"Okay," he said as she handed the device over to him. He set it on the counter beside him and focused on her instead. "And what do you want me to do tonight?"

"Since you're down here you can save me a trip. When you hear me go in to her, warm the bottle and bring it up, then you can give it to her—that's what the rocking chair in her room is for."

"But you'll stay in there, right?" he said, his expression showing no concern but his voice ringing with it.

"Right. Especially if you still can't get her to burp. If you put her back to bed without that she'll be up crying before long and there will have to be a lot of floor-walking the rest of the night."

"Guess you should have taught me better today, huh?" he goaded.

Addie rolled her eyes at him and he smiled at that.

"I don't have a bathrobe," he said then. "Do you want me dressed before I get up there or—"

"Well, you can't come up in the buff, if that's how you sleep!" she said in a hurry, alarmed by that thought.

Or maybe *alarmed* wasn't the word for what was really going through her at the thought...

"I'm not sleeping in the buff here, no," he said, his smile turning a little lopsided and a lot cocky. "I brought pajama bottoms."

But not the tops?

Visions of finding him in a wet T-shirt when she'd arrived home Sunday danced through her head. That had been breathtaking enough. If he came upstairs with no shirt at all... Just the idea boggled her mind.

But what was she going to say? A shirtless man wasn't indecent, and how prudish would she sound if she told him he had to put on a shirt?

It'll be the middle of the night, she assured herself. *I'm only half-awake, I probably won't even notice.*

"As long as you're not naked or in your underwear or something," she said as if she couldn't care less.

And praying to be granted that indifference.

Then she went on, "I do have a bathrobe but I don't take the time to put it on. The goal of the middle-of-the-night feeding is to get in, keep the light dim, the room quiet, do whatever needs to be done, get Poppy fed and burped, then get out so she barely wakes up. The quicker the better. The longer she has to cry before you get there, the longer the feeding takes, the more commotion, the more

awake she'll be and the more risk that she *won't* go
back to sleep."

"Mission-oriented—now you're speaking my lan-
guage," he said, the dress code seemingly no longer an issue.

For anyone but Addie.

"So—" he crossed his arms over his chest "—the
minute I know the game is on, I'm out of bed, bottle
in the warmer, and then straight upstairs with it."

"Right," Addie confirmed.

And since everything was done, they had a plan
for what was to come, and it was getting late, she
opted not to linger and risk any more flashbacks or
unwanted thoughts or images.

"I'll leave you to have your beer if you still want
it," she reiterated.

"Lost the mood," he answered as if something
else was occupying his thoughts.

And that something else seemed to be her, because he was staring pointedly at her face.

Then he said, "Now that I've had a closer look
at Poppy, I've been trying to tell if I can see any of
me or my family in her."

"Can you?" Because she couldn't and she hoped
that that was because there was nothing of him or
his family in Poppy.

"No," he admitted. "Not at all. But I can't see
any of Della in her, either..." His gaze on Addie's
face didn't waver. "It's you she looks like, isn't it?
She has your color hair, the shape of your eyes..."

Addie liked that that was true. Although she had

to admit that if Poppy had to be a Camden she would be lucky to get those blue eyes. "My friend Kelly thinks Poppy looks like me, too."

"Do you think the poor kid will go through that weird-looking thing you did?"

Not expecting him to veer off in that direction, Addie laughed. *"Weird-looking thing?"* she repeated, making it sound like that was news to her.

"All I remember of you from before is that your arms and legs were so long you looked like a spider monkey, you had a mouth full of braces and stringy hair that somehow got caught in them. And as I recall there were some seriously chapped lips for some reason, too," he said with enough levity in his voice not to be overly insulting.

Plus, it was an accurate description.

Accurate enough to make Addie grimace. "Yeah, eleven through about fourteen were not my best years. I have the pictures from then hidden."

Tanner grinned as if he could understand that. But then he said, "Maybe you should un-hide them for some before-and-after—it might offer a lot of hope…"

Addie could feel a blush heat her cheeks at the compliment in that. "For Poppy's sake I'm counting on her skipping that stage so she never needs hope that she'll get out of it."

"Were you afraid you wouldn't?"

"Every time I looked in the mirror."

He was still staring at her, as if he was taking in the details of the changes, applying them to memory.

Then his ultra-blue eyes went to her mouth and he said, "What I didn't understand was the chapped lips...looked like they hurt..."

"It went along with the braces for some reason. And I was a kid, I couldn't keep track of a tube of lip-goo to save my life—I must have lost a hundred of them."

His grin turned into a thoughtful smile that had something different to it. Something more kind and understanding than teasing. Something with a hint of sensuality...

"Looks like they've healed pretty well now..." he observed, his voice softer, deeper...

And maybe even more sensual...

Addie wasn't sure if she was imagining that. Maybe because she was breathing in the scent of his cologne again and it was going to her head.

She told herself it was more likely to be that than what she imagined was happening.

"Well, I grew up," she answered his comment about what her lips were like now, intending to sound matter-of-fact but failing for some reason, because her voice was soft, too. And held a touch of innuendo, although she had no idea what she might be hinting at.

Except that she was looking at his lips, too.

And this time when she flashed back to the previous evening, to his hand around her arm, she also recalled thinking about him pulling her up against his body and kissing her. With those lips that made her believe he'd be good at it...

His arms were still across his chest and she couldn't be sure, but she thought he just barely leaned over them, coming closer.

She told herself to square her shoulders in an off-putting way, say that good-night she'd thought she was headed for, and get out of there.

But she didn't do it.

And worse than that, she felt her chin rise, her head tilt...

But just when she thought it was going to happen, just when she'd given in to the wish that it would, it didn't.

Instead he froze.

Then it was *his* broad, broad shoulders that squared, his spine that straightened and drew him back, putting just enough distance between them again to shut it down before it had begun.

The way *she* should have...

Not wanting him to know there was disappointment flooding through her—or, for that matter, that she'd had any inclination of what he'd almost done—Addie did some damage control.

In her schoolteacher voice, she said, "Nights around here can be tough, so my advice is to get what sleep you can while Poppy does."

Not quite as quick to come completely out of that moment, the best Tanner seemed to be able to muster was a nod.

"So, good night," Addie concluded.

"'Night."

She went to the kitchen table for the laundry basket and the baby monitor receiver she'd kept close since putting Poppy to sleep tonight. Picking them up, she headed out of the kitchen, all under Tanner's still watchful gaze.

He didn't say anything, though. And neither did Addie as she left him there.

But for the life of her she didn't know what was going on between them. They were two people at odds over a baby. How could they possibly have just come close to kissing?

Chapter Five

While Tanner spent Tuesday finishing the repairs to the downstairs bathroom, working on the kitchen outlet and patching the siding outside and the drywall inside, Addie painted her bedroom and connecting bathroom. She managed to finish the hallway and tiny upstairs bathroom, as well, with odorless, lead-encapsulating paint.

After managing to basically avoid each other throughout the day—including for a lunch that she made and that they ate separately while they worked in different areas of the house—at five she cleaned up, took a shower and washed the paint out of her hair, then did a quick blow-dry and left it to fall in loose waves.

Even though she knew she shouldn't take the

time, she also applied a little eyeliner, mascara and blush, trying to deny to herself that the coming evening of Tanner's continuing childcare lessons had anything to do with the extra care she was taking.

She held onto that denial even as she dragged the suitcase she'd packed for her honeymoon out of the closet.

It was full of new clothes she'd bought for the trip.

Clothes she'd intended to return since she didn't end up going on the honeymoon.

Clothes that—as she'd painted today and thought about what to wear tonight—she'd begun to consider keeping.

Not because of Tanner, though, she'd convinced herself despite the need all day to fight flashes of him doing Poppy's middle-of-the-night feeding last night. Only because, after everything that had happened up to this point, it had occurred to her that she'd earned a few new things.

When she'd moved the suitcase from Sean's apartment to the house, she'd thought that it made sense to return everything, because surely she wouldn't want to wear things she'd bought with Sean in mind. But he wasn't really *on* her mind anymore. And as she opened the suitcase and surveyed the contents, she realized she had no bad feelings about the clothes. And no aversion to wearing them.

In fact, she liked the idea of having some things she *hadn't* ever worn for Sean, all of them purchased because she'd thought they had a little wow factor.

For tonight she chose an expensive pair of jeans that she'd indulged in because of their low-rise sex appeal and the cute embroidered flowers on the back pockets.

To go with them there was a short, sheer white peasant blouse that she wore over a waist-length, pink, supertight spaghetti-strapped tank top.

Okay, yes, she'd bought the outfit to be a little tantalizing because it showed hints of her midriff, and no, she was *not* trying to tantalize anyone—or so she told herself. But the outfit was cute and when she put it on she felt like a new woman. She felt her confidence get a boost it hadn't had since the wedding. And for those reasons—and only those reasons—she kept it on and left to pick up Poppy.

She could hear Poppy's cries when she reached the top of the stairs that took her to Kelly's second-floor apartment. Which meant that the entire second floor could probably hear, too.

Addie had to knock twice before Kelly opened the door, and when she did the noise Poppy was making was even worse.

"Uh-oh," Addie said, reaching for Poppy to relieve Kelly. "Has this been the whole afternoon, since I talked to you at noon?" she asked as she went inside.

"This is how she got up from her nap," Kelly answered. "There doesn't seem to be anything wrong—her diaper is dry, nothing seems to hurt, she doesn't have a fever. She stopped long enough to take her bottle. She burped great, there's no gas, but then she started this all over again. It's like she's just in a bad mood."

"I'm so sorry," Addie apologized.

"It's okay. Our resident crab, Mr. Bloom next door, has been banging on the wall—which hasn't helped—but other than that I'm just sorry Poppy's upset."

"Let me take her home before she gets you in more trouble around here," Addie said.

Kelly didn't argue—although it was difficult to talk at all over Poppy's cries. Addie's friend merely packed the diaper bag as Addie strapped the baby into the carrier.

Once the bag was packed Addie took it, apologized again, and told Kelly to have a nice time on her date with her boyfriend, Drew. Then Addie hurriedly took Poppy out to the car.

She agreed with Kelly's assessment that Poppy didn't seem sick or in pain, because almost as soon as she had the carrier snapped into the car seat base and had set the sedan in motion, Poppy quieted.

"You just wanted to go for a ride?" Addie said when silence reigned again.

She glanced in the rearview mirror that reflected the mirror positioned for her to see Poppy in the back-facing car seat. The two-and-a-half-month-old was still wide-awake and had grabbed her squishy giraffe around the neck to suck on the toy's head.

"I'll have to check the book, but maybe even though it's early your gums are bothering you today? Maybe we're having a sneak peek at teething?"

Addie paused, then said, "Or maybe you just knew you'd be going home to more of Tanner's childcare lessons?"

Another pause as if Poppy might answer and then Addie said, "Sorry. I know he's *really* not good at *anything* he does with you, is he? Or maybe you just don't like him any better than I do."

But was that true anymore? Addie asked herself. Because as much as she wished disliking him was as clear-cut as it had been for the last seventeen years, it wasn't.

And the fact that it wasn't was providing her with less of a shield from those moments when she couldn't seem to help noticing his attributes.

But how was she supposed to go on finding fault with him now when he'd worked tirelessly both at Gloria's and around the house? When he was Mr. Organization-And-Pick-Up-After-Himself? When he'd pitched in with the dishwasher and laundry last night even though he could have merely stood by and watched? And even this morning—how was she supposed to disapprove of a guy who volunteered to clean the kitchen of the breakfast mess so she could take Poppy to Kelly?

It definitely wasn't as clear-cut.

Then, too, there was the way he'd handled her setting him up to fail his first tutorial with Poppy yesterday. While another man might have hit the ceiling over it, he hadn't caused any kind of up-roar. Instead he'd used the dead squirrel in the wall to make his point.

"I guess he's not really so bad," she conceded reluctantly to Poppy. "If he wasn't trying to take you... But that's a really big strike against him."

Almost the only strike against him, though...

Addie had to admit that hearing his side of things about Della gave her more to think about. And reason to give him the benefit of some doubt, now that she knew more of the details of what had gone on between the two of them and led up to that afternoon when Addie had condemned him.

His relationship with her sister *had,* after all, only been a high school romance. Teenagers might have fantasies about those things lasting forever, but the odds were against it. And if he'd made it clear to Della from the get-go that college was the cutoff and Della had pretended to agree, then he hadn't led her on—which it had seemed to eleven-year-old Addie that he must have. Plus, he'd suffered Della's hijinks even before her false pregnancy claim—the hijinks of all hijinks. Since then none of the men that Della had dated had stuck around very long.

"There *is* still the way he acted that afternoon," she argued, unwilling to absolve him completely.

Because despite having more understanding now of his detachment then, it didn't make that aspect of him any less of a worry when it meant Poppy could have a lifetime of such emotional distance with him if he didn't connect with her better than he had so far. A lifetime of the effects of a mother who had trained him to be unyielding and cold-blooded.

The thought of putting Poppy under that kind of

rule terrified Addie. So while her resentment of him over his early response to her sister might be giving way, her worry about what kind of father he might be was gaining ground despite his determination to be the dad he hadn't had himself growing up.

"He's not a teddy bear, that's for sure," she said to Poppy. And becoming a tough marine after the way he'd been raised didn't help matters.

There was just so much good *and* bad when it came to him…

"But where was the bad last night when he was *supposed* to be irritated and annoyed like Sean was over the middle-of-the-night feeding?" she lamented. Because just when she'd wanted Sean-like sighs and grumbles, complaints and outright tantrums over the interrupted sleep, Tanner hadn't done any of that. He'd taken it completely in stride.

"It *was* only the first night…" Maybe when he'd chalked up more of them, things would change?

But his stoicism the previous night certainly hadn't bolstered her hope that he'd be scared away by what had bothered Sean so much.

At least he hadn't come upstairs shirtless, she thought as she stopped for one of Merritt's few red lights, recalling the drawstring pajama bottoms and the white tank top he'd had on—the image she'd been trying to chase away all day long when it popped into her head.

The tank top hadn't left him much more than shirtless, though. His oh-so-muscular biceps and shoulders had been bare but it was better than no shirt at all.

Unfortunately, when he'd situated himself in the rocking chair and she'd set the tiny bundle of Poppy in those bountiful arms, against that broad chest that only sported a thin layer of white knit that was partially transparent, it had raised her own temperature.

So much that she'd had to pretend the nursery was unduly stuffy so she could open the window and take a few minutes to stand in front of it to cool off.

All in all, for her, it had been the roughest middle-of-the-night feeding in two and a half months, and she'd been glad when she'd turned from the window to find Tanner again botching the job so she could take over and send him back downstairs.

"But what was it like being up against that chest..." she wondered out loud, her mind lingering on the mental image she still had of Poppy cradled to it...

A horn honking from the car behind her at the stoplight brought her out of her reverie to realize the light had turned green while she'd been lost in her own head.

"I have to do better," she told the baby as she put the car into motion again. "Even if I can't completely hate him, I at least can't have any kind of weakness for him."

And feasting on the sight of him—and what it kept doing to her—was a serious weakness.

Especially when she'd finally been able to fall

back asleep and had dreamed of taking that white tank top off him...

"Even if I can't hate him I have to be impartial," she said with more conviction as she pulled into the driveway, talking now solely—and firmly—to herself. "I have to be unaffected. And I'm going to be!"

She closed her eyes, took a deep breath, held it and worked to cement that vow to herself before she let herself exhale.

Because how horrible would it be, she reasoned, if she actually fell for the guy who could hurt her in the worst way she'd ever been hurt...

"Maybe we should take her into the emergency room."

It was after eight that evening. Within minutes of Addie getting Poppy home from Kelly's apartment, the baby had started crying again. She'd kept at it all evening, except while taking her before-bed bottle and burping well, and cried even harder and more angrily when Addie had tried to put her down for the night.

And it *had* all been up to Addie, with Tanner left as a bystander, because even though she'd intended to keep her word and teach him better how to change a diaper or give a bottle, every time she tried, Poppy only cried more at being in Tanner's inept care. The most that was accomplished was for Addie to show him all the methods and positions to try to calm and comfort Poppy, none of them successful tonight.

As much as Addie wished she could quiet Poppy, she thought it was good for Tanner to experience the reality of a very fussy baby, and she monitored his reaction along the way.

The longer it went on, the more solemn Tanner became. It seemed like he drew up straighter and stiffer as the evening wore on. He said less and less. And Addie began to see what she'd seen in him when her sister had told him she was pregnant— a flat, stony expression, some withdrawal, and he said almost nothing. His suggestion to take the baby to the emergency room was the first words he'd uttered in the last hour.

"You can't take her to a hospital because she's crabby," Addie told him. "I showed you in the baby book what to look for that might mean a doctor should be called and none of that is going on," she reminded him.

"But she keeps at it! And she won't go to sleep— there has to be *something* wrong," Tanner insisted.

"Teething is the likeliest—"

"But you did what the book said about that and it didn't work, either. Is this going to go on all night?"

Now, *that* had some shades of Sean in it, although there wasn't annoyance or anger in Tanner's voice, only indications that *he* was wearing out.

So, more for his sake than anything, she said, "The car ride worked when I got her home today. Why don't we try that? She's already in her pajamas. If she falls asleep we can just bring her home and put her in the crib—"

"And if she doesn't stop in the car we can head for the emergency room," Tanner added.

"Sure, okay, if that seems necessary. But let's just try driving her around first."

"I'll drive," he said as if he needed to be occupied by any form of action at all.

"It has to be my car, though," Addie pointed out. "Because I have the car seat."

"Whatever."

Suppressing a smile at his agitation, she set Poppy in the carrier she'd left near the door, and buckled her up.

"Do you want to see how the seat clicks into the base?" she asked him when they reached her car in the driveway, poking the bear just a little to see how flustered he actually was.

"Not now," he said in a clipped tone, putting her assessment of him at super-flustered and making Addie smile a second time as she put the carrier safely in the base.

When she was finished with that, she stepped back to close the rear passenger-side door and found Tanner bent over the roof, leaning on both forearms, his head hanging between his shoulders.

"Are you okay?" she asked, amused.

"I'm fine," he claimed, sounding anything *but* fine. Sounding as if he was wound tight.

You want to be a dad? This is being a dad...

Addie didn't speak her mind, though, leaving him to reach that conclusion on his own. She merely got into the passenger seat of her car to wait for him to come to terms with whatever it was he seemed to be dealing with.

Maybe this was where it would end, she thought hopefully. Maybe he was having trouble making himself get into even closer quarters with the still-crying infant, and he would decide he didn't want any part of parenthood and just call this whole thing off.

What a relief that would be!

Although, as true as that was for her, there was some other feeling lurking behind it.

Was it possible she might *not* be delighted to see the last of Tanner Camden right here and now?

No, she told herself. In fact, it was so *im*possible that she stopped even considering it. She did, however, lean forward to glance through the driver's-side window to see if she could tell what he was doing.

For Poppy's sake she wanted to get going, and called out to him, repeating, "Are you sure you're okay?"

He didn't answer but he did finally open the door to get in. Except he couldn't, because the seat was too close to the steering wheel.

Seeing it, seeing the tension in those striking features of his, Addie expected—and braced instinctively—for a Sean-like reaction. But Sean had never held it together this long the way Tanner had—a small, simple thing like not being able to easily get into the car would have set him off for sure.

But all Tanner did was release the lever to push

back on the seat until it would accommodate his long legs. Then he got behind the wheel and started the engine.

"Where to?" he asked her, still stilted but without the rancor she would have been in line for from Sean.

"Driver's choice," she said, enjoying the clean scent of soap that lingered from the shower he'd been taking when she'd arrived home.

With the car in Reverse, he pivoted in her direction, putting a long arm behind the back of her seat as he looked out the rear window.

It was the textbook posture for backing up and shouldn't have taken her by surprise. But for a minute, before she realized what he was doing, she thought he was putting an arm around her...

Excitement ran through her like a flashfire until she knew what was actually going on. Then she reprimanded herself.

Of course he wasn't putting his arm around her! Why would he? And if he even tried, excitement wasn't what she would feel, so that couldn't have been what she *had* felt. She must have misinterpreted her own response. Maybe after so many hours of Poppy's wailing she was just jumpy.

She stared out the front window as if she hadn't even noticed. But now *she* was sitting up straighter, stiffer.

Addie's house was six blocks from the heart of Merritt—somewhat farther away than Kelly's apartment and Gloria's house. And just as had happened after she'd set out from Kelly's apartment, Poppy stopped bawling almost the minute they started heading into town.

"Can that be it?" a disbelieving Tanner whispered, checking the rearview mirror.

Addie shrugged. "Apparently she just wants to be in the car today."

"Little bugger," he muttered but there was almost a note of elation in his voice. "We still better drive, though, right? Or she'll just start again?"

"I'd say we'd better drive until she's asleep."

Tanner nodded and his whole body seemed to relax into the seat. It was a much faster rebound than anything Sean had ever done. Sean would have been bouncing between pouting and ranting. And that quick recovery caused Addie to worry that Poppy's fussiness might not have had the full impact on Tanner that she wanted.

They passed through Merritt proper and got on the highway out to the farmland.

"How often does this go on—the crying jag thing?" Tanner asked after a while, when it seemed like he trusted that Poppy wasn't going to start again.

"It happens," Addie said, careful not to let him think it was an isolated occurrence, even though Poppy *was* ordinarily an even-tempered baby.

"I don't know how that much noise can come out of that tiny a person," he marveled. Then, after a pause he added, "It…gets to you…"

"It's how babies persuade you to do what they

need you to do. If it wasn't so grating it would be easier to ignore."

"Oh, there's no ignoring it," he said more to himself than to her.

Addie resisted the urge to say anything else, still counting on the experience making a stronger impression than anything she could add.

It was a balmy, early June night. By then the moon was nearly full and high in a cloudless, starry sky. And only when Addie began to feel it dissolve, did she realize how much tension she'd been carrying herself.

But the drive was serving to soothe her, too, and she decided that maybe she needed—just for the time being—to give herself over to the simple pleasure of the ride through the peaceful countryside.

"This is nice," she said softly, thinking that it had been a long, long while since she'd felt even a moment without burdens. And even as she reminded herself that Tanner was another source of stress and worry, it somehow didn't quite register that he was anything but a big, brawny, great-smelling, awesomely attractive man in the driver's seat.

"It would be nicer if I wasn't starving," he said.

Addie laughed. Poppy had been so demanding tonight that they'd never gotten around to having dinner. "There's the Hotdog House up ahead, next to the drive-in movie," she said.

"The drive-in is still running?"

"During the summer months and they don't show anything but *really* old movies."

"And the Hotdog House?"

"The same—open from Memorial Day until Labor Day, when the drive-in is."

Tanner smiled. "And how about the hot dogs—are they *really* old?"

Addie smiled at his joke. "I think they're fresh."

"Can we risk the drive-through?" he asked with a nod toward the back seat.

Addie craned around to peer at Poppy. "Her eyes are closed...maybe..."

"I gotta try."

He wasn't kidding when he'd said he was starving—he ordered himself four hot dogs to Addie's one, fries for them both, and two bottles of water.

"Uh-oh, eyes are open," Tanner announced when he checked on the mirror images of Poppy as they waited for their food. Luckily, the crying hadn't started again yet when the order came.

But rather than pulling over to eat, they got back on the highway and went farther past the farmland, where it turned into a more tree-laden area.

"We used to come out here and have woodsies at the lake," Tanner said then. "Was that still going on when you got old enough to drive?"

"We didn't call them *woodsies*," she said as if the term aged him. "But we did meet at the lake to hang out. To swim in summer, have bonfires in winter and ice-skate if the lake was frozen solid enough."

"And shoot fireworks on the Fourth of July?"

"When Merritt does such a big display of its own? No."

"Oh, yeah, that's right," he said, tossing her a mischievous half smile, "you're a *girl.* After the town show, a bunch of us guys came out here and shot bottle rockets and cherry bombs into the lake."

"Those are illegal—where did you even get them?"

The half smile turned into a grin before he watched the road again and said, "I'll never tell."

Then he poked his chin in the direction of the food sacks in her lap. "How about breaking out some of those fries while they're still hot?"

Addie opened the bag with the fries in it, dumped both cups directly into the sack and held it out for him to take some.

"Ketchup?" she asked as he did.

He ate what he'd taken, before he said, "Yes to ketchup, and salt those babies, too."

Setting the bag of fries in the console between their seats, she opened packets of salt and did as instructed. Then she squirted ketchup from small packs into one of the cups that had had the fries in it before.

As she did she took a furtive look at him, wondering where this more free-and-easy Tanner had come from. Was the drive releasing it in him? The night air? Or was this some kind of radical rebound from the hours of Poppy's crying?

Addie put the ketchup cup in the cup holder nearest to him and helped herself to a fry, looking boldly at his profile. "You like to drive?" she ventured, wondering if he was one of those car guys who loved to get out onto the open road.

He indulged in three of the hot, greasy fried potato spears at once, drenched them in ketchup and glanced at her curiously. "I like it well enough," he answered as if the question was strange. "Why?"

"You're a different person all of a sudden."

"I am not," he refuted.

"Oh, you so...oo are," she insisted. "It's like you've been let loose."

He shrugged. "I'll admit that I'm feeling kind of like I do when I get back from a successful mission that I was worried might not be successful—like a load has been lifted. Is that what you're talking about?"

It was. But she had to take issue. "In what way did *you* pull off a successful mission tonight?" she demanded.

"I'm the guy at the wheel, aren't I?"

"Oh pleeeze..." she said facetiously. "You could barely even make yourself get in the car."

Rather than deny that, he laughed. A deep rumble she liked more than she wanted to.

Then, with obvious false bravado, he said, "I've been screamed at nonstop by drill instructors from hell aiming to grind me down—you think a crying baby got to me?"

"*I* got in the car. You didn't," she goaded.

He smiled this time, conceding her point. "I'm here now."

"Huh," she huffed, wondering if the more free-

and-easy Tanner would stick around or if the *marine* would make a reappearance.

Tanner glanced in the mirrors once more and changed the subject. "Eyes are closed again. Are you gonna have to feed me hot dogs while we drive all night or do you think we can stop?"

That still sounded like the free-and-easy Tanner.

"The only way we'll know is to stop and see what happens," she answered.

This time he pointed his chin straight ahead. "Potter's Point is coming up. Shall we try?"

"Might as well. Maybe we'll at least be able to eat a little before we get back on the road."

Tanner gave her a sideways glance and the mischievous smile returned with a hint of wickedness to it. "In my day," he said, as if accepting her earlier implication that he was old, "Potter's Point was the prime make-out spot."

"Yeah, that's never changed," Addie informed him.

"Think you'll be able to keep your hands to yourself if we park up there?" he joked.

"I'm sure it'll be a trial for me, but let's risk it," she said jokingly, hiding the fact that a hint of titillation did skitter along the surface of her skin at the idea of parking with him. Especially since she couldn't help recalling that kissing him had crossed her mind twice—and that last night she'd thought it had crossed his, too.

Tanner turned right onto a well-worn dirt road that took them to the top of a mesa. She saw a half dozen other cars parked in no particular order except with space between them for privacy.

He stopped near the edge of the mesa, where no other cars were parked, giving them a panoramic view of Merritt in the distance.

Addie again craned to see into the car seat while Tanner used both mirrors for the same purpose.

"So far, so good?" he whispered.

"Give her a minute..." Addie whispered in return.

But when Poppy didn't stir, Addie said, "Maybe we're okay..."

As if testing it, Tanner rolled down his side window and again they both waited to see if the sound roused the baby.

When Poppy still didn't make a peep, Addie opened the sack of hot dogs very cautiously and took out two of the five that Tanner had ordered with extra mustard.

"Do I leave the engine running or not?" he asked.

"We can't let it run and waste the gas. I know my tank wasn't full when we left."

"Then it goes off..."

He turned the key in the ignition and once more they waited to see if that woke Poppy.

Since it didn't, Addie passed Tanner his hot dog and opened her own to take a bite.

"Oh, I needed that!" Tanner whispered after downing half the dog.

The rapture in his tone made Addie laugh. "They're good hot dogs but not *that* good."

"You don't know how hungry I am."

She was, too, which did help to enhance the taste of the ordinary hot dogs.

They ate in silence until he'd gone on to his second one.

He was looking out the windshield at the lights of Merritt when he said, "Huh... I never noticed how good it looks from here. Peaceful. Not like it could erupt any minute in chaos and ugliness."

Was that what he might ordinarily be on the lookout for at a vantage point like this? Addie wondered.

But there was too much of a sense of contentment in the car for her to want to ask.

"Maybe I'm just getting a new appreciation for old Merritt," he mused.

Then he took his third hot dog out and repositioned himself in the driver's seat, bracing his back against the door to face Addie.

"So what kind of a teenager did you turn out to be? Cheerleader? Party girl? Bookworm? Tomboy?" he asked in a hushed but closer-to-normal voice.

"I wasn't like Della—I wasn't a cheerleader. I was a lot shyer, sit-in-the-back-row-and-hope-nobody-noticed-me—"

"Until the braces came off and then you must have wowed 'em."

Addie laughed. "Hardly. I don't think I've ever *wowed* anybody."

"Me," he said matter-of-factly.

"I wowed you?" Addie asked with a voice full of doubt about that, not reading too much into it. "Is that because after the braces and chapped lips and stringy hair you didn't think there was any way I'd come out looking human?"

"Well..." he said in a teasing tone, as if anyone would have thought that.

"Now that I think of it, I did get one *wow,*" she added when it occurred to her. "The first day of sophomore year, the braces had just come off, and Andy Brenner said, *Wow, those braces were really ugly. You're lucky you finally got them off.*"

Tanner laughed but grimaced sympathetically. "Lot of tact, that guy," he judged.

"Andy was never Mr. Smooth. Were you—at fourteen, fifteen?"

"Probably not," he confessed. "I'd had a couple of girlfriends by then but it was all pretty awkward."

"You had girlfriends before Della?"

"Sure. Della was the last in Merritt, not the first."

"Really..." That was an interesting morsel of information. Somehow Addie had never thought of that.

"Sure," he repeated.

"You were a player?"

He laughed again, starting on his fourth hot dog. "Nah...it was just the way those things go. I had a couple of grade school crushes, one on my fifth grade teacher but she didn't reciprocate..."

"Good thing."

"I didn't think so," he countered with more humor. "Then there was the friend of a girl Quinn liked when we were in seventh grade—he paid me to go to the movies with her so the girl he liked would go, and I hit it off with the friend. I liked my lab partner in eighth grade biology, so I asked her to the dance that was coming up, and then I didn't dance with her, I just horsed around in the gym with my friends. So that was a flash in the pan. When Stacy Harrold moved to town I got assigned showing her around school and—"

"You showed her around more than school?"

"I tried," he said with a grin.

Looking at him, Addie realized that she must have had tunnel vision to think of him only being with Della. That dark hair, those blue eyes... Of course he'd never had any problem getting girls.

"How about you and boyfriends?" he asked then.

"I told you, I was shy."

"So none?" he said incredulously.

"Not none, just nothing noteworthy."

"But there *were* boys..."

"Not during the braces phase. Not really any for about a year after that—even though I was sure the braces coming off was going to change my life. It was a huge letdown," she said with some humor of her own despite the fact that it had been incredibly demoralizing to find there wasn't any immediate change in her appeal to the opposite sex. "I did get asked to the homecoming dance sophomore and senior year—"

"Not junior?"

"Nope. And they were just one-and-done dates."

"And proms?"

"Junior year the track coach set me up with his

pole-vaulter—a really sweet guy who I didn't like as anything except a friend, even though he somehow got the idea we were instantly boyfriend and girlfriend," she confided with another laugh. "But I did get asked, on my own, for senior prom the next year. By *two* guys," she bragged with another laugh.

"Ah…you were just a late bloomer," he said as if he had the explanation to something. "How about your first kiss, though—that didn't take until you were a senior, did it?"

"No. Just until the braces came off."

"Did it happen up here or somewhere else?"

"Somewhere else. This was *not* a first-kiss spot. Or was this where you had your first?"

His smile was devilish. "Kiss? Nooo. My first kiss was with Sharon Kinney in the barn when I was eleven."

"But this was where you had a different *first*?" Addie pried.

The smile stayed devilish. "Would you believe it's where I had my first beer?"

"You didn't have your first beer at a *woodsy*?"

"I just said would you *believe* this is where I had my first beer, not that I did…"

"Very funny," Addie chastised again but she did laugh once more. "And I'm guessing that I don't want to know what first you *did* have up here."

"It was really my first shot of tequila."

She thought he was still joking, but regardless she was enjoying their banter as much as she'd enjoyed the drive up to Potter's Point, and didn't mind that he was toying with her. It was just nice to still have the free-and-easy Tanner in play, nice to be getting an image of him that was putting Della further and further at a distance from him.

"Did *you* have your first beer at the lake?" he asked then.

"I did."

"And the first time you came up here?"

Addie laughed. "The *only* time I came up here was with Leanne Dryer. She was dating Jude La-Dune—"

"I knew the LaDunes—they were bad news."

"Jude was two years older than us. Leanne had heard a rumor that he was cheating on her. She wanted me to come with her to see if he was up here and if it was true."

"Was it?"

"It was. But she flashed a flashlight into four other cars before she found him and that was how I learned that a lot more than kissing went on at Potter's Point…"

"You didn't know that from personal experience."

"Which you would have…" she said just to needle him.

"I'll admit to a little," he hedged. "But there were also some trips up here to wreck it for my buddies or my brothers—boys will be boys, you know. Sometimes a wingman, sometimes…not," he said with a smile that looked like whatever things he'd done to wreck someone else's rendezvous here were the more fun memories.

"I just avoided this place after the time with Leanne. I was afraid that agreeing to coming up here was agreeing to more than I was willing to do."

Tanner's grin was crooked. "So you never got the Potter's Point rite of passage?"

"Nothing before college was on that level."

She'd finished eating and had begun to use the empty hot dog sack for trash after Tanner had taken out his last one. He only made it halfway through the fourth before apparently reaching his fill, because he discarded the other half then.

He offered her what was left of the fries, but when she declined he disposed of that sack and what remained in it, too, adding it to the trash.

Since they were both done, Addie opened her glove compartment for the mints she kept there.

She'd been sitting partially turned toward the console before. But when she found what she was searching for and sat back, she was facing Tanner more than she had been. Just in time to watch him uncap his water bottle and take a long drink that exposed his Adam's apple and the underside of his jaw, where a jagged scar was hidden.

"Oooh...that's quite a scar..." she blurted out, shocked by it.

"It's nothing. Happened a long time ago. Mishap on a mission," he downplayed, sounding all marine again.

Wondering if she'd lost the free-and-easy Tanner, she offered him a mint. "Dessert?" she said lightly, hoping to lure out the more laid-back Tanner again.

He accepted one and by the time she'd taken one for herself his handsome face was contorted.

"Geez! These things should come with a warning," he complained of the strong mints she liked.

"When it comes to green chili you can eat fire," she reminded him.

"That's different," he claimed, flinching. But he didn't spit it out. Instead he leaned his head slightly through the open window behind him and tried to see into the car seat.

"I think she's still out," he reported.

But just when Addie thought he was going to suggest they head back into town, he settled and focused solely on her, seeming relaxed again.

Another mischievous smiled danced on his lips. "I want to feel bad that you never had any of the Potter's Point...*entertainments*...that I did," he said, picking up their conversation where they'd left it. "But I kind of like that you didn't..."

"That sounds suspiciously like a double standard," she pointed out.

"It does, doesn't it?" he said. But he didn't take it back. He just went on studying her as if there was something about her he was seeing for the first time.

"Seems strange that we knew each other but we don't really know each other," he said then.

He was right—she'd known him as Della's boyfriend, as one of the actors in the ugly play Della had staged, but that was really the extent of it. Now she was *getting* to know him, and seeing him with more dimension than she ever had before.

"It does seem strange," she allowed. "But I suppose it's true, isn't it?"

"Now that a long time has gone by and we're no longer who we were back then…" He paused as if to let that sink in. Then he said, "Think there's any chance of you and me wiping the slate clean of the past?"

Before tonight, maybe not, Addie thought. But now that she was seeing him through a broader perspective that was beginning to encompass the whole man rather than her memory of him…

"I don't know. Maybe."

Wiping the slate clean of the past didn't change what still might come. Or any of Addie's feelings and fears of losing Poppy. She needed *not* to forget what she'd seen in him seventeen years ago, in case it was still at the core of him and could impact her niece.

But on the other hand, they each *had* grown up, matured. He'd become the man she was beginning to see tonight.

And recognizing that they were no longer kids, that they were each just getting to know the other as adults, and going on from here as if they'd only recently met rather than carrying too much old baggage seen through a much narrower view, did seem like a better idea. A wiser choice than hanging onto that old baggage and that much narrower view that wouldn't leave her with a clear image of the person she might have to entrust Poppy to.

"Can we at least give it a try?" he asked when a few minutes had lapsed as she thought about it.

"Okay..." she conceded.

He smiled like he was grateful. "Good..." he said quietly, seeming to find some satisfaction in her agreement, as if it genuinely mattered to him.

In a way, that seemed to add a hint of vulnerability to this Tanner she was seeing tonight, and as heady as his obvious strength and power and masculinity were, a little vulnerability increased his appeal.

Dangerously, since it launched her into thoughts of kissing yet again...

There was heat coming from those electric blue eyes that stayed steady on her, studying her, seeming to appreciate what he was looking at, and there was a charge in the air between them.

Maybe it was Potter's Point, Addie thought. Maybe it was just something in the atmosphere up there on the mesa, because if ever there was a place that cued kissing, this was it.

And when Tanner began to move ever so slowly forward, she didn't retreat. She wanted him to kiss her.

He hesitated with his face inches from hers, as if to make sure he wasn't crossing a line, and she tipped her chin. And made him smile again, this one slow and sexy.

He raised a hand to the side of her face, cupping it, caressing it as his eyes delved deeply into hers, searching them—again as if for signs to go ahead or not.

Addie arched up enough to close more of the distance between them without initiating the kiss herself, because she wanted *him* to kiss *her*.

And then he did. Softly at first, his mouth only lightly on hers, chastely, respectfully, for a brief minute, before that kiss ran away with itself and took them along...

His lips parted and there was more pressure, more of a presence. Addie welcomed it, contributed to it, parting her own lips in answer, tilting her head to let it happen.

And oh, how it was happening.

Being kissed by him, kissing him, was like no other kiss she'd ever indulged in, and she wasn't even sure why. Their mouths were just a perfect match and nature took it from there to make it an impeccable kiss.

A kiss that went deeper and deeper until their mouths were open wide enough for his tongue to come calling. For hers to meet it and greet it and lead it on a rowdy spree as if this wasn't their maiden voyage. As if somewhere something far tamer had led up to it and given them knowledge and familiarity and license to let loose something they'd been containing.

His hand went from her face to the back of her head to brace it for more. More that was sensual and enticing.

Both of Addie's hands went up into Tanner's

coarse hair, then down his thick neck to those shoulders and that strong back that didn't flinch even when her fingers dug a little into it.

His other arm wrapped around her and pulled her to his chest. Her breasts pressed impudently into the stone wall of his pecs while she became increasingly aware of him holding her superbly tight.

And the only thought that ran through her mind was *more, more, more.*

Then she thought about the baby in the back seat... And knew she had to curb this before any more, more, more went on.

She pulled her arms from around Tanner and laid her palms to his chest. Wishing like mad that it didn't feel so good to the touch, she forced herself to push against it as she sent her tongue into a reluctant withdrawal and drew her mouth from his, too.

"There must be something in the air up here," she said, trying for a light tone but finding only a seductive-sounding whisper.

Tanner got the idea, though. He eased away ever so slightly but moved his hands to barely grasp her upper arms, to squeeze just one gentle squeeze before he let go and smiled a dazed smiled down at her.

"Must be," he said, his own voice raspy with what had erupted between them.

"We could probably head home..." Addie said. "I think Poppy's asleep enough..."

Tanner nodded, still gazing into her eyes as if there was something he couldn't let go of yet.

Then he seemed to put some effort into it, sighed

with acceptance, and took his hands completely away, turning to face the steering wheel again. He started the engine but didn't put the car in gear, looking out the windshield once more.

Addie watched the marine in him come to the forefront then. She saw his posture straighten, his head go high, and everything lock into place.

Only this time she was glad to see it because she was having so much trouble keeping herself from restarting what she'd stopped. She needed to know one of them could summon some trustworthy resolve.

Neither of them said anything as they left Potter's Point, and as Tanner drove them home.

Neither of them said anything as they took Poppy inside and up the stairs to the nursery where the baby remained sound asleep as Addie put her lovingly in the crib.

It was only when Tanner stepped out of the nursery doorway and Addie joined him in the hall outside the door she soundlessly closed behind her that their eyes met again. And held.

Addie wondered if Tanner was going to kiss her again because the same things were between them, in the air around them, that had been there just before he had earlier.

And even as she was hoping he would, she was telling herself she couldn't let him.

She just didn't know if she was capable of resisting...

But apparently that marine resolve was still intact because he didn't move any nearer, or reach for her this time.

Instead he said, "You *have* wowed me, you know. Big time. And I'm in trouble because I don't know what to do about it…"

She felt much the same way but she didn't say it because it seemed that admitting she was in a similar boat might get them right back where they'd been at Potter's Point. Only with her bedroom right next door. So all she did was nod.

"But I'll keep trying. I wouldn't want you calling my grandfather on me," he said, part promise, part joke.

"I do have him on speed dial," she countered without any threat at all.

For a moment they stayed there, lingering in a lack of certainty, on the verge of what they were both fighting.

Then Addie found something inside of herself that let her turn away and leave him there in the hall.

She heard him turn in the opposite direction and head down the stairs just as she reached her room and went into it.

But once she was behind her own closed door she realized that tonight she'd begun to understand something with an all new clarity.

There was a whole lot to Tanner Camden that could make him impossible to forget.

Chapter Six

"Thanks for these," Tanner said to his brother Micah early Wednesday morning. "Addie needs a new roof, but with this many shingles I should be able to patch the worst of it and buy her some time."

"Glad to help. They were just extras we weren't sure what to do with," Micah said as Tanner closed the truck's tailgate. "Lexi's already at the bakery but she left me a full pot of coffee—go sit on the porch and I'll bring two cups out."

Tanner noted that his brother wasn't issuing an invitation as much as just telling him what to do and he wondered why.

But regardless of the reason, Tanner said, "I should get back and start on the roof."

"You have time for a cup of coffee," Micah insisted. "And you look like you need it. Go sit," he finished with an older-brother order.

Tanner thought the shingles had earned Micah that much, so he shrugged, shut the tailgate and followed his brother to the front porch.

"Morning coffee on the front porch? Are you turning into Big Ben?" Tanner asked along the way.

Big Ben was what they frequently called the grandfather who had helped raise them. It was the habit of Ben Camden to have his breakfast and coffee on the front porch whenever the weather allowed.

"It's not a bad practice," Micah answered. "It's actually kind of a nice way to usher in a civilian day. Besides, the kitchen is on the side of the house that the tree took out when it fell. I have a buddy in there rewiring today. Better that we talk out here."

"Do we need to talk about something?"

"Just sit. I'll be right back," Micah said.

On the porch there was a small white wicker table with two matching wicker patio chairs on either side of it. Tanner passed up the first one and the table, sitting on the chair farthest from the front door while his brother went inside.

He didn't know what was up with Micah but he had to admit that just sitting there felt unexpectedly good.

Early-morning country air.

The quiet.

The sense of the day just starting.

It all helped him calm down some inside...

Micah returned with two steaming cups of black

coffee. He handed Tanner a mug and then took his own with him to the other wicker chair. "Did you get the DNA results?" Micah asked, propping his mug on the arm of his chair.

"Not yet."

"I thought maybe you did... So if it isn't that, what's going on that has you so quiet and looking like your best friend is on life support?"

Tanner let out a mirthless chuckle at the description that probably fit even though he hadn't realized he was being unusually quiet or glum—apparently the reason for this sit-down.

"Are things not going well?" Micah reiterated before Tanner could answer.

"Last night was rough," he confided. "The baby was on a crying jag for no reason anybody could tell. Hours and hours and hours of it from the afternoon on."

"All through the night?"

"No, but... The crying caused the sleepless night but not because it was still going on—when nothing else stopped it we put her in the car and took a drive to see if that would get her to doze off—"

"Did it?"

"Yeah. Thank God. And she stayed asleep until the middle-of-the-night feeding. But still..."

"Are you getting up to do the middle-of-the-night thing?"

"I'm getting up but so far me actually doing it isn't working out. I'm all thumbs with that stuff and last night we didn't want to have to go out driving around again at two a.m."

"But the crying shook you up so much you couldn't sleep?"

"It freaked me out...left me up worrying even once it was over."

Worrying one minute.

Thinking about that kiss at Potter's Point the next.

Fighting how damn bad he'd wanted more of that...

"What were you worrying about?" Micah asked.

"Oh, hell, Micah..." All the thoughts Tanner had had through the night came rushing back to unsettle again. "I'm not good at any of the baby stuff even when things are going all right. But yesterday? There was just no telling what was wrong or why she was crying. She wouldn't stop, and I didn't have any idea what to do. I thought we should take her to the emergency room—"

"Was she sick?"

"I didn't know. Why would the kid scream like that if she wasn't sick or in pain or...*dying*?"

"That bad, huh?"

"You don't know," Tanner said, concealing none of the effect it had had on him.

"But you didn't take her to the hospital?"

"No. Addie wouldn't do it. She read in some baby book she has and there was none of the criteria—no fever and I don't know what else—"

"The crying didn't get to Addie?"

"Maybe. But she stayed calm. I don't know how,

but she did. She just kept walking around, jiggling Poppy, swaying with her, rocking her, patting her... I can't even remember all the things she tried."

"You didn't try anything?"

"Like I said, I'm all thumbs. Every time I took her, she just cried more and I gave her back to Addie. The only idea I had was the emergency room."

"I don't know...that seems logical to me," Micah said in a commiserating tone, obviously without any more experience or knowledge of babies than Tanner had.

"It's a good thing we didn't. When nothing else worked Addie decided we should try to take the drive. She humored me by promising to go to the emergency room if the crying didn't stop then—"

That made Micah smile sympathetically. "Were you freaking out enough to *need* humoring?"

"I was trying not to show it but Addie's pretty sharp, I don't think I fooled her. I didn't know that something like just driving around might do the trick, so that never occurred to me. I didn't know about any of the things Addie tried before she did them last night. I don't have a clue what to do at the best of times. So when it was all said and done, and the worst was over, and I tried to go to sleep myself, I started thinking what if I was alone with that baby and something really did go wrong with her? If she's mine and I step up for that, could I screw something up and do her harm?"

Micah started to say something, but before he

could, Tanner cut him off with another thought that had driven him out of his bed.

"Plus, you don't know what it takes just to do the everyday things, or how little sleep you get. I can handle a few nights—training took care of that. But for weeks or months on end while I still report for duty? How the hell am I supposed to be a single parent *and* do what I do? What about the well-being of my men? Could I screw something up there, too?"

"Okay, okay..." Micah said. "Slow down. You don't even know yet if you *are* the dad, and in your head you're already risking the lives of your men— that's a big leap."

Tanner didn't have a response to that. He might have been—he might still be—spinning out of control, but his concerns weren't unwarranted. He was responsible for the lives of the marines under his command, and if he became a single father he'd be responsible for Poppy's life, too. He might be getting ahead of himself but both things were very real concerns that he couldn't ignore.

"Remember that you're over at the Markham place to *learn*," Micah pointed out. "That's training—just like any other training, just like recruit training and infantry training and special ops. You go in green, you come out knowing what to do. Last night might have been the Crucible."

"Little sleep, little food, a lot of marching, hardship—the test to see if you *are* trained, if you can put your training to use. Get through that and you're a marine. If last night was that, I did *not* pass the test..."

"Because it came at the *beginning* of your training instead of at the end of it. Think of this as getting a taste of the worst, a preview. You just started. You'll get better."

Even if he got better, he still didn't see how he could do it all. Tanner shook his head. "It's such a freaking mess..."

"It'll get better."

"Or worse if I really am the dad," Tanner grumbled fatalistically. "I can't believe I got myself into this."

"I don't know that you got *yourself* into it," Micah muttered in response.

"I should *never* have gone anywhere near Della again. I should have known she could have had a scheme..."

Micah didn't dispute that. He merely said, "Water under the bridge, man. But what about Addie Markham? She's supposed to be teaching you what to do—is she not doing that? Is she leaving you hanging out to dry while you help her with that house?"

"No, no, no, it's not like that," Tanner said, a little surprised at the level of protectiveness that rose in him at his brother's critical-of-Addie tone. "She was hard on me the first time—she shot everything at me too fast to learn. We had to come to some terms, but she's..."

She was so many things Tanner wasn't sure where

to go with that. But thinking about Addie rather than Poppy did help his doldrums for some reason.

"She's taught me what she's been able to teach me since then. I can make formula and there's a lot of laundry and I know *how* to change a diaper and give a bottle—I'm just really bad at anything hands-on. I don't think she likes me—"

"The baby or Addie?"

"The baby—Poppy," Tanner clarified.

Although when this began it *had* seemed as if Addie disliked him, too. But he was getting less and less of that impression now. Especially after the last two nights...

Like on Monday night—he'd wanted to kiss her, he'd come close to kissing her, but he'd pulled back at the last minute. But in retrospect, he thought she would have let him, although he wasn't entirely sure of that, because he hadn't really been able to tell if she was daring him to try or freeing the way for him.

But then there was Potter's Point...

He wasn't left with any more thoughts about her hating him, after *that* kiss.

"You probably tense up and she senses it."

Micah's voice penetrated Tanner's mental meandering, and all he could think was: *there was nothing tense at Potter's Point. Potter's point was off-the-charts great.*

Then, belatedly, he realized his brother was talking about his lack of skills with Poppy and he refocused.

"I definitely tense up when it comes to Poppy,"

he agreed. "She's so damn tiny I'm afraid I'll drop her or break her or something. Addie says I just need practice but then we hit yesterday and last night and there was no chance for that—there has to be optimal conditions for me to do anything."

And sometimes he didn't want to. Sometimes he just liked watching Addie with her.

It did something to the pit of his stomach just watching her hold that baby as lovingly as she did, cuddling her, talking to her, giving her a bottle and looking down at her with such joy.

He didn't understand it. It wasn't something he'd ever experienced before. But it happened. Every time.

"Addie's a good teacher but I don't know how I could ever be as good as she is with her," he said then. "I told you, not even the crying got to her. And she had me to deal with on top of it. But she was a rock."

"She's not high-maintenance like Della was—"

"Not so far," Tanner said. Although he was still reserving judgment, still on the lookout for that.

"So she really is trying to teach you, but you're just a klutz at it?"

"Yeah."

"And other than the baby stuff…are you getting along with her?" Micah asked.

Tanner took a drink of his coffee and then held the mug with both of his hands around it, stalling before answering so he could respond indifferently. "We get along."

How that tipped off his brother, Tanner didn't know. But Micah raised his mug to his mouth, and rather than taking a drink, he laughed over his cup at him as if he'd seen through the show of nonchalance.

"Just how well *do* you get along?" Micah asked and then sipped his coffee, eyeing Tanner suspiciously from under his brows.

Tanner still tried to sound casual. "We get along fine. There's no problem keeping up conversations. She's funny. She's a good sport. She's fair, reasonable—when I called her on giving me a hard time she copped to it. She's kind of girl-next-door but…" *Too mind-blowingly-beautiful to be just that…* "But she's my old girlfriend's little sister," Tanner said as if that made everything else insignificant.

"So what?"

So wasn't that weird? Not that it seemed weird when he was with Addie.

Alone, together, talking to her, she was all new to him. She was just a smart, interesting woman he was getting to know. And liking more and more as he did. She wasn't anybody's shadow; she was her own person, separate from anything and anyone else.

She was just Addie, with that long, silky, burgundy-colored hair he wanted to bury his face in.

She was just Addie, in those low-slung jeans yesterday with the flowers on the back pockets riding a rear end he'd wanted his hands on.

She was just Addie, in that flowy, see-through white shirt that had tantalized him with hints of the tight tank top underneath it. The tight tank top that had flashed about an inch of flat stomach here and there that had been pure, sexy temptation...

"You don't think it matters that she's Della's sister?" he said.

"I think it matters if she's...*like* Della was. Or if you like her because she reminds you of—"

"She doesn't. Not at all." Which might be part of the problem. If he saw anything of Della in her he'd be immune, especially at this point, when he'd potentially been *twice* burned by Della.

"And you *do* like her," Micah concluded as if he'd only been guessing before.

"There's nothing *not* to like," Tanner confirmed, still trying to keep his tone objective.

Micah nodded as if he was learning more than Tanner was saying, regardless of how Tanner said it. "So, what if the baby *isn't* yours? Will you just figure you dodged the bullet, put Addie and this whole thing behind you, and go on, business as usual? Or is there so much to like about Addie that you might not want to do that?"

Coming into this situation, he'd definitely figured that if the baby wasn't his he would have dodged a bullet and he'd go on with his life.

So why didn't he feel as if he had that same easy answer at the ready? If he wasn't Poppy's father, why *wasn't* he so eager to take off without a backward glance?

It would be a much easier answer in terms of Poppy. She'd stay with Addie, who loved her and wanted to raise her.

It would be a much easier answer for Addie, too. She'd go on with her life the way she'd intended before he came back to Merritt to throw a wrench into the works. She'd adopt the baby she loved.

So how come it wasn't such an easy answer for him anymore?

"Addie's a hometown girl with mile-deep roots here," he said, thinking out loud. "She has a life here, a job here, friends here. I'm a career marine, with other obligations."

And the fact that kissing her last night had made him see stars was irrelevant.

But again, why didn't it *feel* irrelevant? Why the hell would the thought of him just being set free again have any complications to it? Why would the idea of *that* bother him now?

"I'm just all over the place," he grumbled.

"And the gloom is back..." his brother observed.

"I like things clear and straightforward. And nothing is that right now."

Although one thing was: even at that moment he was itching to get home to Addie, wanting to see her.

Talking to Micah was bringing up more feelings in him than Micah realized and Tanner just couldn't take it right now.

He set down his coffee cup and stood. "I really need to get going, get to work on that roof."

Micah nodded, not trying to detain him again. "You know I'm rootin' for you—whatever comes of this," he said.

Tanner had the sense that his brother saw the

chaos in him but since there was nothing he could do to help, Micah was merely giving him what support he could.

"Thanks," Tanner said brusquely—not because he was upset with his brother but because he was upset with himself. "And thanks again for the shingles."

Micah nodded and Tanner went down to his truck, leaving with more confusion than he'd brought with him.

Wednesday was a new day for Poppy. She woke up in good spirits, and there were no signs of whatever had caused the previous day's lengthy wailing session, or any repercussions from it. In fact, as Addie dressed her after breakfast, she cooed for the first time, which was about the sweetest thing Addie had ever heard.

After taking the baby to Kelly, Addie returned home. Tanner was working on the roof by then and didn't see her. Not wanting to call attention to herself, she went inside to paint all the doorframes and baseboards upstairs.

She stopped work just before two o'clock to take a shower and to shampoo her hair, paying close attention to her clothes, hair and makeup afterward.

Tanner and that kiss just weren't the *only* reasons for the extra care with her appearance today.

The job she'd assigned herself for this afternoon was also part of it. She was returning wedding gifts. And she wanted to look as if she'd completely recovered from her wedding that wasn't. Which, she had. With every passing day she was more and more relieved that Sean was out of her life.

She just had to convince everyone of that, to get across the message that there was no reason to give her the sad faces and sympathies. Their pity was actually what embarrassed her more than being dumped by Sean.

She hoped that doing her hair and makeup, and wearing cute new clothes would convince her well-wishers that she had let go of Sean. That being left at the altar was over and done with. And that they could all put it far, far behind them.

Today she chose a sleeveless yellow jersey surplice top from her honeymoon suitcase. It was bright and cheery. It crossed diagonally to her left hip to form a V-neck high enough to leave a little to the imagination but low enough to get that imagination going, and she hoped that helped make it clear that she was in no way pining for Sean. That she was moving on.

The kiss came to mind again. That kiss last night meant she'd definitely done some moving on.

But it shouldn't have happened. And it most certainly shouldn't have happened with Tanner, she told herself. Although, in the course of moving on from a long-term relationship, rebounding wasn't unheard of.

The more Addie thought about kissing Tanner in terms of a rebound, the more light dawned for her.

Not only did rebounding explain her wanting to

kiss him the night before and then doing it last night, not only did it explain the strength and speed of her attraction to someone so unsuitable for her, but it also took away some of what made it feel like such a big deal. It was nothing more than a rebound!

And rebounds just happened, they didn't mean anything real. They didn't last, they just served their own temporary purpose to help move on. So last night's kiss had merely been a purpose-serving kiss. Even if it had turned her to mush.

As much as she'd relived that kiss, she'd berated herself for it. It was reassuring to realize it wasn't anything more than a rebound thing.

But still, it probably shouldn't happen again. Not that she wanted it to. Not that she would let it even if he tried.

Would she?

"Just get back to business," she said out loud when she realized how much time she'd just wasted thinking about Tanner and this situation with him again. Time during which she still hadn't chosen pants.

She sighed and refocused her attention on the contents of the open suitcase, recalling that she'd bought a pair of black hip-hugging clamdiggers to wear with the surplice top.

After putting on the pants, she chose flat honeymoon sandals that exposed the wedding-day-eve pedicure that was no worse for wear. As she was slipping her feet into them it occurred to her that the shower downstairs was running.

Patching the roof was no small job, so it didn't make sense that Tanner was done with it and would be showering. He'd even worked through lunch and merely had her climb the ladder to bring him sandwiches for lunch.

If he had something else to do this afternoon he hadn't told her about it even when she'd informed him of her own plans. But his business was his own. She wasn't his keeper, after all.

Leaving it at that, she flipped over to brush her hair from the bottom so it was at its fullest and shiniest, and used a pale pink gloss on her lips to go with the other makeup she'd applied.

One final check in the full-length mirror to be sure that there was nothing about her to make her seem mopey, and she went downstairs.

The shower had been off for a while by then and just as Addie reached the entry and pivoted around the banister, Tanner stepped out of his bedroom door into the hallway.

His almost-black hair was still damp, the scruff of beard that had shadowed his face earlier was shaved clean, and he smelled of that soap she liked almost as much as his cologne.

He clearly had *something* to do, she thought at that first sight of him, because a pair of tan cargo pants and a tight, dark navy blue, short-sleeved crewneck T-shirt had replaced the tattered and torn workpants and ragged sweatshirt he'd been wearing to work on the roof.

"Give me just a minute and I'll be ready," he said

when he spotted her, using the hand towel he was holding to roughly dry his head.

"Ready?" Addie echoed.

"I thought I'd go with you," he said without pre-amble. "Didn't think this was something you should have to do by yourself."

When she'd climbed the ladder to bring him his lunch, she'd told him she was going to return the wedding gifts later this afternoon. She *hadn't* told him how much she was dreading it, or hinted that doing it by herself made it all the worse.

But to have company and reinforcement? He had no idea how much better it made her feel not to have to face this alone.

"You're sure?" she asked, thinking that being backed up by one of Merritt's hometown heroes would likely also take some of the interest away from her and put it on him—sparing her any extra helpings of pity, the way it had with Gloria.

"Let's just get this done," he answered, tossing the hand towel into the bathroom and leaving his hair naturally tousled and much sexier than it should have looked with such slapdash care.

And all Addie could think as they started to carry gifts out to her car was that sometimes the man was hard to hate…

Having Tanner along to return wedding gifts was a huge benefit. As everyone accepted their present back, there was always the question about how Addie was doing, an utterance of sympathy for the situation, and several assurances that returning the gift wasn't necessary.

But those exchanges were brief before the much bigger elephant in the room was addressed—Tanner.

It was as if she was taking him on a door-to-door welcome-home tour. Everyone was thrilled to see him and to have a moment of catching up with him. It was even taken in stride that he was with Addie, because—while there was no indication of whether or not gossip had announced that he might be Poppy's father—word *had* spread that he was helping repair her grandmother's old house. That inspired a number of her family friends to thank him for that as well as for his service to the country.

All in all, having him along rounded out the edges on the worst of the chore for her and before she knew it, her car and trunk were empty and they'd accomplished it.

Feeling as if one more burden had been lifted— and the last of them that had anything to do with Sean and the wedding—Addie picked up Poppy from Kelly's while Tanner was waylaid by an old acquaintance in the apartment's parking lot.

With the evening in front of them and Poppy also in a good mood, Addie suggested they have a concentrated session of baby care lessons.

And between the relief of being able to wash her hands of Sean and the wedding, and the gratitude she felt for Tanner's assistance that afternoon, Addie even managed to suspend her own qualms about losing Poppy to him and offered patient and generous instruction this time.

He still wasn't adept at any of it, but he did essentially do all the hands-on care, including diaper changes, bath, bottles, and getting Poppy to bed.

"Did you hear that burp?" he whispered proudly to Addie as they left the nursery.

"I did," she whispered back, silently closing Poppy's door.

"You didn't even have to step in and try for another one."

"Are you thinking you're ready to go solo?" she challenged as a hint of her fears niggled at her again.

"Not by a long shot," he answered.

His obvious trepidations calmed hers, even as she reminded herself that not only was she keeping her half of their agreement tonight, but that she also owed him for the moral support and distraction he'd provided today.

And in the vein of owing him for going above and beyond their agreement, Addie insisted on treating him to dinner.

Grocery delivery had long been a perk provided by the General Store, usually to the local elderly or ill. But tonight Addie used the convenience herself—ordering two steaks, salad fixings and the last loaf of the market's own homemade bread.

When she told Tanner what she was doing, he suggested he go out to the farm to *borrow* a bottle of his grandfather's red wine.

With a sense that there had been some small victories today to celebrate, Addie agreed.

While Tanner was gone and as she waited for the grocery delivery, she did the nightly baby chores. She was just finishing with them when the teenage delivery boy arrived.

After exchanging a few pleasantries and tipping him, she unpacked the bag.

Then she seasoned the meat, put the salad together, made the dressing and set the kitchen table. The steaks were broiling when Tanner got back and ready when the wine was poured.

"This is a lot better than hot dogs from a roadside fast-food joint," he said as they sat down to eat.

"I wanted to say thanks for today," Addie told him. "Having you there did help."

"I'm glad," he said simply.

It was the food they talked about through dinner—what they were eating and noteworthy meals they'd had before. Since Tanner was far more traveled than Addie was, she asked where in the world he'd had the best—and worst—food, and that took them through the entire cleanup.

Which would have been the ideal moment to say good-night.

But instead Tanner held up the wine bottle to judge how much was left, and said, "We didn't even make a dent in this—I know we'll have to get up in a few hours but what would you say to a little more?"

She said okay despite knowing she shouldn't—

and they took their two replenished glasses with them to sit in the living room.

The floor was the only seating option, so Addie sat with her back against the wall in the corner where the moonlight beamed through the big, un-draped picture window and landed in a bright white square—the only illumination in the room.

Tanner followed her, using the wall that formed the other side of the corner as his backrest and al-most facing her.

"You need some furniture," he commented as they settled.

"This was your idea," she pointed out.

"Yeah, because the light from that full moon makes this place look…not as bad…"

Addie laughed. "But it still doesn't look good," she interpreted his pause.

"I'd say you're a ways away from that yet, yeah."

She couldn't argue with the truth and instead de-cided to continue their conversation about his life since he'd left Merritt. And maybe expand on it to soothe some of her own curiosity.

"So those fancy dinners you've had in far-off places… Were they dates?"

He laughed. "A time or two."

"That's it? You've had two dates in the last sev-enteen years?" she joked.

"Maybe three," he said, going along with the gag.

But Addie wanted details and she refused to be deterred. "Seventeen years is a lot—you could have been married and divorced in all that time…" That had just occurred to her. Now that it had, she realized that although she'd asked before if he was currently married or involved with anyone and knew he wasn't, she hadn't asked if he'd *ever* been married. "Have you been?" she asked.

"Have you?"

"I'm the one who can't get to the altar, remember?" she answered facetiously.

Tanner took a drink of his wine, then apparently decided to stop ducking her questions. "I've never gotten to the altar, either, no."

"Ever been engaged?"

"Haven't ever even considered it," he said without hesitation. "I haven't been in anything serious enough for that."

"In all these years?" she exclaimed, wondering if widespread playing around had taught him the skill in that kiss last night. And not particularly relishing that idea.

"I've only been serious about my career," he said as if it had to be one or the other.

"But not about *anyone* since Della?" Addie persisted in part amazement, part disbelief.

Tanner didn't immediately respond. He bent one knee to support his forearm, his hand dangling his wineglass over his shin before he finally said, "After Della I laid down some strict rules for myself when it came to females and to being a marine. And I've stuck to them."

"Rules," Addie repeated.

"I've dedicated myself to the Marines. I've put everything into that."

"The way your mother taught you."

He shrugged one of those impressive shoulders. "It's what's gotten me where I am."

"Okay. But still, don't try to tell me there haven't been women in your life," she said in a you-can't-fool-me tone.

It seemed to amuse him that she wouldn't let him skirt the issue of relationships, and maybe because of that he gave in. "Romance has not been high on my priority list," he said. "Yes, there have been women, but since I followed the rules I set for myself, nothing has gotten too serious."

"Is that the purpose of your rules—to keep you from getting serious about anyone?"

"No," he said as if he didn't know how she would have come up with that.

"So it sounds like there are two sets of rules. Being a marine is number one for you and you won't let anything distract you or throw you off course. That's the marine set of rules, right?"

"Right."

"And then there's a separate set of rules about women? What are those?"

"Were you always this nosy?" he asked.

Addie figured that was just another evasion. "I'm only gathering background on you," she said matter-of-factly and as if she had every reason and right to.

His handsome face screwed into a pained look

that made it clear he was reluctant to get into the details of his rules about women.

"Come on, spill it," she commanded as if she had the right to do that, too.

"The rules about women are about the *type* of women I steer clear of..."

"And what type is that—tall, short? Redheads, no redheads?"

"It's not about looks, it's about...other things."

"Rich? Poor? Influential? *Not* influential? What?"

"I don't care about any of that, either. But I do care that whatever a woman does is important enough to her to keep her life from revolving around me."

Okay, Addie liked that he didn't expect to be the center of any woman's universe.

"The rules aren't extreme. A woman just has to be low-key," he went on. "She has to be even-tempered. Steady, stable. Practical. Levelheaded. There can't be any drama."

Ah, so that was why he'd tried to avoid getting into this.

Addie said what she thought he was trying to keep from saying. "If there's any sign that someone is like Della, you steer clear."

His face pinched up again. "I didn't want to be that blunt."

"But yes," she finished for him.

His expression confirmed it.

She wondered what the relationships he did indulge in might look like.

"Okay, so you meet someone and if you like her and she's *low-key* enough and has a job she's really into, and she accepts that you being a marine comes before she does, it might last a while?"

"It might," he allowed.

"Why doesn't it get serious and last forever?"

"Well, a lot of reasons," he said with a shrug. "I've had a few relationships where the woman *seemed* to fit the bill at first, but then *wasn't* so... low-key."

"Meaning what?"

"Meaning that after a while they wanted more than I could give, and got emotional about it and—"

"The first time a woman you're dating gets emotional you're out the door?" Addie asked.

"No drama, remember?" he reminded of that portion of his rules, as if that justified it. "But most of the relationships I've been in haven't gone there because they've been with women who are...well, like me. Their career came first, too. Military usually, but some not, and the lion's share of their energy went into that. We've had some fun when we both had time for it, but eventually one or both of us relocated or got too busy, and things just fizzled out, so we've gone our separate ways—"

"Without any *drama*?" Addie added.

"Without any drama because nobody's been in too deep."

"That is very neat and tidy," she commended sarcastically.

"For me that's the best kind of relationship," he contended, as if it was merely common sense.

Addie wondered if she was seeing what she thought she was seeing. "So you don't ever want a real, long-term relationship," she surmised, again worried what that could mean for Poppy, since raising a child definitely qualified as that.

"A *real, long-term relationship* isn't against the rules, no," he said as if he didn't know what she was getting at.

"But how do you think you're going to ever find a real, long-term relationship if the woman you're with lets you know she wants more, but you interpret that as temper and drama and end it? And the women you prefer are the ones where both of you are just passing time with each other and aren't actually invested in anything but your careers? It seems to me that your *rules* are making sure you *don't* ever get into anything serious, let alone get married."

He frowned at her again, narrowing his eyes to add a glare to it, but with humor rather than menace. "What are you thinking, Markham? That I'm setting myself up for relationship failures?"

"What I'm thinking is that my sister really kind of messed you up."

That must've taken him by surprise, because he laughed once more, wryly this time. "Actually I've always thought that she taught me a valuable lesson," he refuted.

"I don't know… It looks to me like she left you so gun-shy that you made up a bunch of *rules* to make sure you never really get close to anyone," Addie argued.

That seemed to take some of the levity out of their conversation. Tanner took a drink of his wine and then stared at the glass, not responding.

Addie didn't know if he was considering what she'd said or if she'd gone too far and made him mad.

Thinking that maybe the wine had caused her to be too outspoken on this subject, she rolled slightly onto one hip to set her glass on the floor, out of easy reach so she didn't drink any more of it. Then she sat back against the wall, somehow ending up a few inches nearer to him than she'd been before.

He still hadn't said anything and just as she convinced herself that she'd stepped out of bounds and should apologize, he sighed and said, "I wouldn't say I've been *gun-shy*, I've just been…selective. And it's worked out for me. I've been close enough to the women I've been involved with—"

"Close enough?" she repeated his words. "What does that mean?"

"It means I've been comfortable—"

"But that you hold back? That you don't ever jump in with both feet?" Addie guessed.

"I suppose," he said as if he didn't see anything wrong with that.

"And whoever you're with—the ones that don't

crash and burn right away by showing any kind of emotion? Are they holding back, too?"

"I don't know… Maybe…probably…other things come before I do, so—"

"And that's okay with you?"

He looked at his glass as if he'd had enough of the wine in it and then did much the same thing Addie had. He put it far away from him on the floor behind him, clearly deciding not to drink any more before he answered her question.

"Now that I think about it, it's more okay with me than the relationships I've had where the women *did* jump in with both feet," he answered with candor.

"The ones who were emotional," Addie reiterated.

"Pretty much."

"Oh, you are so gun-shy," she accused with a small, sympathetic laugh that said he was clueless.

This time he shrugged it off rather than deny it. "Call it whatever you want. Like I said, the situation with Della taught me a lesson."

"I don't like to say anything against my sister, she was my *sister*…" But oh, what damage Della had done to this guy. "I know she was a handful, and with you she pulled out all the stops. And you weren't much more than a kid, so it makes sense that it left an impression." She paused, unsure how he was going to take what she was about to say. "But it's one thing to learn a lesson, incorporate it into the way you do things or the way you look at things.

It's good if it opens your eyes. It's something else if it warps your life."

"*Warps* my life?" he took a turn at parroting her. "How do you figure my life has been warped?"

"You haven't let anyone get genuinely close to you since then. You've made sure you haven't gotten genuinely close to anyone else. It seems to me that you've hidden behind your career for the last seventeen years, and that makes me a little afraid for you—"

"You're afraid for me?" he asked as if that was the most ridiculous thing he'd ever heard.

"It makes me afraid you'll die alone..." *Even if you end up with Poppy...*

And what would it do to Poppy if Tanner did prove to be her father, took her away but then raised her without ever getting close to her, either?

"Well, that's grim!" Tanner joked.

He was referring to her comment about him dying alone but the thoughts that had come into Addie's mind after she'd said it had struck her as doubly grim. Which made it all the more important to her to show him the error of his ways so he could possibly correct them before they could do any damage to Poppy.

"It is grim, but you're making a joke out of it because you're trying to blow me off instead of considering that I might be right," Addie countered.

Tanner arched his full eyebrows at her. "You think me being a marine is just *hiding out*? That deep down I'm a shivering coward?"

"I think you use being a marine as an escape hatch when it comes to your personal life. Because yes, deep down I think Della left you scared silly of relationships. I think that the *only* reason you got anywhere near her eleven and a half months ago was because she convinced you that she was completely over you the same way you've been completely over her for years. Because she convinced you that she could take you or leave you the same way you could take or leave her—or any other woman you've let get anywhere near you since Della's lie."

"Deep down I'm *scared silly*?" he said, taking issue only with that part of her suppositions about him. "It takes a lot of guts to say something like that to me."

"It's true, though, isn't it?" she accused seriously.

Tanner grew more serious, too, his handsome face sobering, leaving Addie certain he was going to tell her this was none of her business, to butt out.

She waited for it. For quite a while, because there was a fairly long silence before he said, "I haven't thought about any of this like that…but…maybe… I know there weren't any feelings on my part eleven and half months ago and I sure as hell wouldn't have done what I did if I had thought there were any on the other side, either."

That was better than *Mind your own business*. It just wasn't good enough. Not with Poppy's future on Addie's mind.

"And what about any of the rest of the women you've been involved with?" she asked, forcing the issue. "It sounds to me like you could take or leave any of them, too. That's the way your rules are set up—"

"Okay, yeah, you have a point."

"But you can't just say *maybe* or that I have a point and then just ignore this! You *need* to think about it. You *need* to fix it! Because if—heaven help me—you *are* Poppy's father you *can't* just get *close enough*. You *can't* keep her at arm's length. You *have* to jump in with both feet and be as committed to her as you are to the Marines."

Addie realized she'd ended up showing a whole lot of that emotion Tanner didn't like. But it didn't matter whether or not he liked her; it was Poppy's well-being that mattered. Addie continued to hope she would somehow end up raising Poppy but since the adoption attorney had opened her eyes to the odds of that—like teaching Tanner how to care for the baby's everyday needs should he end up with Poppy—Addie felt she couldn't ignore the relationship side either.

Tanner was studying her intently but there wasn't anything in his expression that revealed if he was put off or angry, or worse.

Then his brows arched again, he sighed, and it was as if his shields came down. And for the second time, she saw some vulnerability in him.

"Okay, you're right," he conceded. "If Poppy is mine I will have to do better. I will have to do something different than I've done when it comes to relationships. I hadn't thought about this stuff but I will. I'll think about that along with everything else I need to think about."

He seemed to mean that and it helped reassure Addie that she'd made some headway on behalf of Poppy. But she regretted that their conversation had put such a damper on the evening. An evening that she'd been enjoying.

Tanner might have been having the same regret, because he switched positions so that his weight fell on one hip and he was angled more in her direction, again bending a knee to use as an armrest.

Then he gave her a sly, sidelong glance and changed the subject. "So one kiss and you're doing a background check on my past relationships? What does that say about you?"

Addie laughed and returned to that earlier joking, teasing vein. "One does not have anything to do with the other. It's Poppy I'm thinking about."

"Mmm…" he mused doubtfully. "And you want me to believe that kiss didn't have anything to do with it."

"Farthest thing from my mind," she lied.

"Funny, I haven't been able to *stop* thinking about it," he informed quietly.

"You *should* stop thinking about it. I'm not your *type*," she reminded him flippantly.

"You *do* get a little riled up and that does mean I'm breaking a lot of rules here." He paused, met her eyes with his blue ones and added in a hushed voice, "So how come I can't help myself and I want to do it again so damn bad?"

"I don't know…" She'd intended that to be glib, too. But her own voice had a breathy come-hither quality to it.

Tanner moved slightly nearer. "Does that mean you *don't* want to do it again?"

He reached out and ran his fingers up her bare arm and the goose bumps he caused with that light touch gave her away. Because the truth was that she wanted him to kiss her again so much she could hardly stand it. That she'd wanted him to kiss her again so much since they'd left Potter's Point that there hadn't been a minute when the idea wasn't lurking behind her every thought.

And now that he'd asked, now that she knew he felt the same way?

She told herself to shut this down, not to let it happen again. And she *knew* she should. But it was refusing herself—and him—that she couldn't make herself do…

It's just a little rebound thing…

"I *have* been wondering if it was just a fluke," she heard herself say.

"A fluke that it was as good as it was for a first kiss?" he clarified.

"Well, yeah."

"Hard to say unless we have something to compare it against. Want to give it a test?"

Rather than answer him—or play innocent—Addie leaned forward until she was a scant inch from him, tipped her head slightly to one side and kissed him somewhat clinically, as if for testing purposes.

Only briefly, though, before she broke it off and aloofly lied again, "That's what I thought—overrated."

Tanner grinned again. "Oh, you did that so wrong."

"Are you saying I'm a lousy kisser?" she said in a mock huff that issued yet another challenge tonight.

"You're a *great* kisser. But that is *not* the way it was last night."

"Really?"

"I think it was a little more like this…"

He slipped his hand along the side of her neck and up into her hair to cup her head as he inclined his in the opposite direction and met her lips with his.

Soft, tender lips parted and kept the kiss light until she was kissing him back. But as soon as she was, it became a kiss every bit as good as the Potter's Point kiss.

Just before it got even better.

As if there hadn't been any interruption, their mouths were open wide again and their tongues were reacquainting themselves, hungry for the renewal of the dance, but savoring it, too.

Tanner's free arm went around her and brought her up against him again, leaving Addie to sluice her hands along the contours of his biceps to his broad shoulders and over them to his rock-solid back.

The kiss only deepened then, and actually improved on the first one as their mouths fused in that same perfection.

The hand splayed against the middle of her back gave her a skilled massage that excited and relaxed her at once. And then dropped to the base of her spine, pulling her closer still before it skipped down to her calf left bare by her clamdiggers.

It was nothing and yet the grip of that big hand around her leg, the feel of his skin pressed to hers, was somehow unbearably erotic, and sparked in her that feeling that had ended the previous night's encounter when she'd wanted so much more.

Only, tonight it didn't make her shy away. Tonight, *more* was all she could think about.

She wanted that big bare hand higher, on her thigh.

She wanted that big bare hand on her side.

On her breasts.

Just for starters...

She still had a tiny voice of reason that told her it was *not* a good idea.

But she didn't—couldn't—listen to it. All she could think about was the phenomenal union of their mouths and that kiss, which was erupting needs in her like none ever before.

There was just something about Tanner. Not only the stellar handsomeness of his face. Not only the appeal of all those muscles, of that fabulous body.

It was almost as if they shared some kind of instinctive bond outside of themselves. Something that was primitive, primal. And impossible to deny.

Being with him, the nearness of him, the touch of his hand, brought everything inside her to life and then supercharged it so she couldn't resist exploring the wonders of it, learning what more she was capable of feeling, of experiencing.

His hand finally meandered from her calf, taking the path she'd wished it would until it rested on only the outermost swell of her breast.

But merely the outermost swell was not where she wanted it. So she turned enough so that it was the fuller side of her breast that brushed his hand in invitation.

He didn't miss his cue, repositioning and taking that already aroused globe completely into his grasp.

Her nipple instantly became a hard pebble as his strong fingers caressed her flesh.

But only over her shirt. Over her bra. Over too many impediments to what she was yearning for.

Even as she expanded into his grip and did her own part in escalating that kiss, even as her own hands delved into his back and gave a hint of demonstration, she was wondering if he realized that the V-neckline of her shirt could provide better access.

But maybe he hadn't noticed. Or didn't realize she was giving the go-ahead.

She sent her own hands to the bottom edge of his T-shirt and eased underneath it, intending only to give him a hint of what she wanted, but discovering that having her own palms against the warm satiny skin of his naked back was a delight all its own, making her briefly forget what she was angling for him to do to her while she just relished that new sensation.

In the process they somehow slid down from the wall and she realized after the fact that they were lying on the floor.

Which was even better.

She lost his hand at her breast then so he could reach down to her thigh and pull her leg over his, bringing her up closer still, front to front.

The length of her body ran the length of his and that set off a whole slew of new feelings.

And just as she was absorbing it all he returned to her breast, this time finding his way inside her neckline, even inside the cup of her bra.

It was everything she'd hoped for and the hint of a moan that escaped her was revealing.

Gentle but not too gentle, his hand was big, warm, strong. Adept and agile, he knew just the right amount of softness and firmness to raise her to even more delight. He knew when to use feather strokes and when to do tiny pulls and pinches of her nipples that sent the most delicious chills along the surface of her skin.

Maybe too delicious, because she felt her leg tighten over his hip without ever having that intention, and before she realized what she was doing, not only were their bodies merely together, hers was suddenly so snuggly aligned with his that she knew without a doubt what this was doing to him.

But she might have gone too far, because with one last squeeze of her breast he released it, replacing her bra and shirt before his hand did a retreat to her upper arm, and that oh-so-carried-away kiss eased into a simpler, lingering one.

Just before it stopped, Addie felt him straighten his back to stretch himself higher than she was.

He drew a breath that expanded his chest and when he exhaled, he dropped his face into her hair. "I'm too close to the edge of no return..." he whispered.

Maybe that was all right...

But something in his tone kept her from saying it.

"And that's it for me," he added definitively. "Until you've had a chance to think...in the cold light of day, with a clear head..."

Addie sighed, dropped her face just enough for her forehead to rest in the crevice between his pecs, and hated him a little for being so right.

But she *was* carried away, and while every inch of her body, her being, demanded that they finish what they'd started, a small rational part of her wasn't absolutely sure they should.

She nodded her head and reluctantly removed her hand from under his T-shirt.

He complained of the loss with a groan but once she was no longer holding him, he rolled to his back, leaving his arm to pillow her head but not touching her in any other way.

Still on her side, Addie looked up that arm to his sculpted face in profile. His eyes were closed and his sharp jaw clenched as if he was working hard on an internal struggle. She gave him a minute, watching him, taking in every detail and trying desperately not to want him, to gain some control over herself.

But lying there with him didn't aid that cause, so she sat up, pulling her knees to her chest and clasping her arms around them.

"The wine?" she said softly as an excuse.

He shook his head, his eyes still shut. "No. I just want you."

Oh, God, she just wanted to straddle him and get it all going again.

She held her breath to fight the inclination until she thought she'd regained some amount of a grip on herself. She knew she had to get out of there, away from him, or this was going to have the end he was trying to avoid.

She got onto her knees and kissed that bicep she'd been lying on before, then stood and went upstairs without so much as a backward glance. A backward glance that she knew would only make leaving him more difficult.

But even once she'd reached her room, gone into it and closed the door securely behind her, her thoughts were still down on that floor with Tanner.

Which was precisely where her body was screaming for her to be.

Chapter Seven

The following day and night were productive but difficult for Addie.

She and Tanner had done Wednesday night's 3:00 a.m. feeding almost wordlessly before Addie finally got any sleep. When she woke up at seven this morning she was hoping that she'd slept away the needs and feelings she'd taken to bed after the kiss on the living room floor. But no such luck.

So, while Tanner worked on the roof all day Thursday and she did a thorough cleaning of the hardwood floors to prepare them for sanding, she went over and over in her mind all the reasons it was good that he'd stopped them before they made love, and why they should never have gotten as close to it as they had.

She reminded herself that he was her sister's old boyfriend. And even if that was long ago, and even if she did have a better understanding of his side of things from that time, it didn't change the fact that Tanner could still be that same distant, detached, reserved person he'd been then. The same person who had disappointed and disillusioned starry-eyed, eleven-year-old Addie. The same person who could still display those elements that she didn't want in Poppy's life and certainly didn't want in her own.

She reminded herself that he was still the one person who could make her worst fear come true by taking Poppy away from her. That essentially made him her enemy. Someone to keep her distance from.

And Tanner himself wasn't the only problem.

As she worked, she reminded herself that she'd just come out of a long relationship. She'd just been left at the altar, dumped unceremoniously. Humiliated.

And yes, even though not marrying Sean had been a relief, the further she got from the wedding that wasn't, the more self-analyzing she did. The more she began to wonder—to worry—about why she hadn't measured up enough to keep Sean from straying.

Sean, who had initially chased her tirelessly even when she wasn't interested. Sean, who had given every impression that he was enthralled with her. Sean, who had seemed to have far deeper feelings for her than she'd had for him. Until he'd won her over and settled in with her.

What was she supposed to make of that? It certainly wasn't a confidence booster.

Compared to Tanner, Sean was bland, provincial. He hadn't traveled the world, expanded his horizons, experienced the exotic, sought out risk and adventure. If she'd bored someone like Sean, what would she ultimately do to Tanner?

She also couldn't discount that she'd had an awful last year and a half, she reasoned with herself as she cleaned floors. She'd watched her parents decline until she'd ultimately lost them. She'd lost Della. She'd become a single parent. And while she loved Poppy no end and wanted to raise her, she had to recognize that instantly taking on the responsibility of a child was still a shock and an enormous adjustment she was only in the process of making.

She'd been running on autopilot much of the last year and a half, maybe not really making good, sound, well-thought-out and wise decisions. Otherwise she probably wouldn't have agreed to marry Sean in the first place. And that had proven disastrous.

She may still be on autopilot, which was a prime setup for doing something else seriously stupid. For making a mistake she might regret for the rest of her life.

By the end of the afternoon, when Kelly brought Poppy home on her way to dinner with her boyfriend, Addie concluded that the best thing to do right now was to stay on track and play it safe. Which meant taking a lot of backward steps when it came to Tanner and returning him to the beware-of list. It meant sticking with a great big fat *no* to letting anything else happen between them.

Then the evening came.

Tanner finished the roof and showered.

And while they ate the stew Kelly had provided, and talked only about the house and what they'd accomplished during the day, Addie actually had moments of breathing only shallowly so she could limit her intake of that clean soap scent of him that she liked.

She kept her eyes on just about anything else to resist feeding on the sight of him, and she told herself to be grateful that he kept the tone simple and friendly, even though she missed the joking, teasing, flirting that had been so much more fun. And so much more dangerous.

But it was the hours after that meal spent in childcare lessons that became the hardest test. Lessons that showed improvement in Tanner's comfort level with Poppy, and in the way he took care of her.

But in the process, Addie watched her baby in Tanner's big, tender hands. Hands that were so careful to contain the strength Addie had felt in them, as the recipient of that touch she still wanted so much.

Watching Tanner feed and rock Poppy, Addie couldn't *not* look at those muscled arms making a hammock for the baby against his T-shirted torso. She couldn't *not* see him hold Poppy high on one or the other of his broad shoulders, where Poppy nuzzled into that thick neck as he gently patted burps out of her.

As the evening went on Addie saw Tanner finally win over Poppy the way he'd begun to win over her. She watched Poppy accept and respond to him, grasping the long index finger he offered her, even granting him one of the rare coos she'd just learned to do.

Something in direct conflict with her greatest fears formed within her: a totally uncalled for sense of the three of them as a family. A warm sense of sharing Poppy with Tanner as she watched the two of them together in the way she'd hoped it would eventually be with Sean.

Inch by inch, all the reasoning she'd accomplished earlier in the day was gone. The small amount of peace that she'd achieved, the small amount of control she'd convinced herself she had went out the window.

By the time they put Poppy to sleep in the crib, Addie was hanging on to her willpower by a thread.

Still, she managed to talk to Tanner only about his progress with Poppy as they did the baby chores.

It helped that Tanner remained merely friendly and polite as they performed the tasks. Had he made any overture at all, Addie knew she would have caved.

But he didn't.

So when everything was finished Thursday night and Tanner did nothing but say a simple good-night before he disappeared into the guest room, Addie climbed the steps to her own room, trying to find comfort in having successfully not jumped his bones,

But never in her life had there been anything more difficult for her to do…

"Here you are, in that fabulous dress we bought for your honeymoon, having a fabulous-hair day, all the color back in your fabulous skin—probably from a little excitement in your life that *isn't* awful. You've had a miserable run for the last year and a half, you've gone through the whole thing like a trouper, you had less sex living with Sean than you could have had just dating around, and now one of the most gorgeous guys I've ever seen in my life is panting after you—"

"I don't think he's *panting* after me," Addie told Kelly as they sat on a park bench in the town square.

"I haven't heard anything that says he isn't as hot for you as you are for him. And as far as I'm concerned, that's a gift from the universe to reward you and you better not look a gift horse in the mouth. No one I've ever known has earned a little mindless, rebound hookup more than you. And when I take Poppy home with me five minutes from now, you're going to be alone with the fabulous-looking Tanner who you're fabulously attracted to. Do I really have to tell you what to do? Because if I do, then here it is… *Do it!*"

Addie had caught her friend up on what had been happening with Tanner—the kiss at Potter's

Point, the steamier near miss in the living room on Wednesday night, Thursday's just-friends day and evening followed by more of the only-coworkers mode today.

She'd also been honest about her own thoughts and feelings. Along with everything running rampant through her. And her reasons for not acting on any of them.

Her friend had responded with the *fabulous* tirade.

But Addie still had doubts.

Friday night was Merritt's Summer Kick-Off Festival. The entire town square had been turned over to it. There were booths selling food, liquor and many homemade crafts, along with a few carnival rides and games. A band was setting up to play for the dance that was about to begin. Couples were gathering around the make-shift dance floor at the base of the town square's centerpiece—a bronze statue of Merritt's own most-honored war hero and marine, General Robert McKinnon.

When Addie took Poppy to Kelly first thing Friday morning, Tanner had gone to rent a floor sander, and he'd been working by the time she'd returned.

She'd spent the day following behind him to clean up the dust that was left, but even though she'd been as thorough as she could, she'd asked Kelly to keep Poppy overnight tonight—Poppy had had a small respiratory issue at birth and Addie didn't want to risk her breathing in anything lingering in the air.

When the sanding and cleaning were finished this

afternoon, Tanner had suggested they take Kelly up on her idea that Addie and Tanner meet Kelly and her boyfriend at the festival.

Addie had thought an open-air social event was better than anything that involved being alone with Tanner, so she'd agreed.

While he brought the floor sander back to the rental shop and then came home to shower, Addie had gotten herself ready.

She'd showered and shampooed her hair—taking special pains to get all the sawdust out of it and to make sure it fell in soft, full waves so she could let it hang free.

Tonight she'd opted for a dress from the honeymoon suitcase.

Yes, she'd questioned the wisdom in that. But she'd purchased the sundress with exactly this kind of evening in mind—an outdoor summer night festivity. And while jeans and tops were a mainstay of her wardrobe, after today's dusty, grimy, gritty job, she'd just wanted to feel like a girl again tonight.

So she had on the flowered, figure-skimming A-line dress that hit just above her knees, with its scoop neck and hand-painted buttons at the shoulder of each strap.

And okay, yes, for the first time, she'd also dipped into the honeymoon underwear.

Which she had no way of justifying. She'd just wanted to.

Tanner and Kelly's boyfriend, Drew—whom Tanner had been friends with from high school football and had reconnected with tonight—had gone to wait for the drawing for the sports car and left Addie and Kelly alone. Poppy had needed her bedtime bottle, so the two had found a free bench near the dance floor.

It was the first real opportunity in days that Addie had had to talk to her friend at length.

Looking down at the baby in her arms, Addie saw that Poppy had fallen asleep, so she put her in the stroller so Kelly and Drew could walk with her back to Kelly's apartment.

"What about all the reasons I gave you for *not* doing it?" Addie responded to her friend's *fabulous* rationalization, referring to the list she had outlined for Kelly—all the things she'd told herself so she could stop thinking about going ahead with Tanner.

"They are all valid reasons. Every one of them," Kelly said. "Ignore them."

Addie laughed.

"I mean it—give in!" Kelly advised passionately. "*Do it, do it, do it!*" she repeated. "Just don't take it for more than it is—a rebound romp, a temporary fling, whatever you want to call it—"

"A one-night stand?"

"Or maybe two or three nights, who knows..." Kelly hedged. "As long as you go in knowing it isn't forever, that it isn't the beginning of anything big. And like I said, no one deserves it or has earned it more than you! Sean chipped your confidence—you don't talk about it but I've seen it in you. And let's face it, nobody gets left for someone else and doesn't come out with some insecurity."

It made a certain amount of sense to Addie. She'd been aware of more self-doubts since being left at the altar, that was for sure.

Or maybe she was merely looking for justification when it came to Tanner...

Kelly spotted Tanner and Drew headed their way then and stood, taking the stroller from Addie. "I'm giving you a whole night free—use it well!" her friend said firmly. "It'll make a new woman of you!"

Addie merely laughed again and shook her head. "Call me if you need anything."

"I won't need anything," Kelly assured as she went to meet Drew, turning sharply to the left to go off in the direction of her apartment.

That left Addie to watch Tanner's approach.

And this time her gaze didn't waver—unlike her attempts *not* to look at him *too* much after Wednesday night.

For the first time since he'd interrupted her at Gloria's house loading wedding gifts into her car, he was wearing dressier clothes—a pale blue pinstriped button-up shirt with the long sleeves rolled to his elbows, and dark blue pants with a brown belt and matching brogues.

He was clean-shaven and his hair was artfully disarrayed just enough to look polished and casual at once. And yes, Kelly's assessment of him as fabulous-looking couldn't have been more accurate.

Even in the shirt that didn't accentuate his muscles galore, he was still an impossibly handsome man.

"Did you win the car?" she asked him when he reached her.

He smiled. "I was just six numbers off," he answered as if that hadn't put him far from success.

Addie was about to make a joke about that but at that same moment there was a noticeable hush in the crowd milling around. She thought the band was probably stepping into place to begin playing, but when she shot a glance to the corner of the dance floor, where the local group had been setting up, there were only idle microphones and instruments.

"Is something happening?" Tanner asked, checking out what was going on, too.

And that was when Addie saw the cause of the initial hush. The cause of the whispers that were now following it.

Among the couples gathering in anticipation of the dance was her former fiancé.

And her former wedding planner.

Everyone in the small town knew Sean. Everyone in the small town knew Addie. She couldn't imagine that everyone who hadn't been in Gloria's backyard that awful day didn't know about it by now. And since so many of those *everyones* were there, since so many of them had come over to say hello or have a look at Poppy or had waved to her and knew she was there, they recognized an awkward situation when they saw it.

For the first time it occurred to Addie that she

probably should have been on the alert for encountering Sean. She'd known all along that he was due back the previous Sunday—she'd made sure to be moved out of his apartment by then. But she'd been so busy and so occupied with Poppy, so occupied—and yes, preoccupied—by Tanner, that Sean just hadn't been in the forefront of her thoughts.

As a result she was unprepared. And there he was, not that far in the distance, and here she was. With so many people watching...

People who had seemed to be veering away from feeling sorry for her. Until this.

But now she was the center of attention again as eyes went between her and Sean, and she even overheard a few uh-ohs.

"Really, what's going on?" Tanner reiterated.

He couldn't piece it together because he didn't know Sean, who had moved to Merritt long after Tanner was gone.

So Addie had to fill him in. "It seems my ex is home from 'our' honeymoon. With the wedding planner. That's them across the dance floor. He's—"

"That skinny blond guy?"

"That's him. And she's the tall brunette next to him in yellow."

That was all Tanner seemed to need to know. He turned his focus instantly on her and her alone. "Are you okay?"

Was she? The shock was wearing off, but the embarrassment of being left at the altar was back, and she wasn't sure what to do or how to react.

Then she took a breath.

She reminded herself that she *had* thought about the long range of living in the same small town with Sean, that she'd considered how to handle it in general.

She'd reasoned that holding a grudge, not speaking to him, entering into some kind of cold war with him would only be uncomfortable. That it wouldn't serve any purpose.

And not only wasn't it the way she wanted to live, but when she factored in that *not* marrying him— while it had been humiliating—had been more of a relief to her than a crushing disappointment, acting as if it *had* been a crushing disappointment seemed silly.

Besides, since the wedding fiasco, she'd hated being the injured party, and she'd hated all of the well-intentioned sympathy that had come with it. How could any of that be put behind her if she didn't prove once and for all that she could rise above being left at the altar?

And here was her first chance to set the tone that said they could be civil.

Recalling Tanner's question about whether or not she was okay, she finally answered it.

"I am," she said, meaning it and liking the sound of it, the truth to it. "But I'm going to go give everyone something new to talk about…"

She headed across the vacant dance floor, aiming for her former fiancé and his new girlfriend.

Sean had apparently not noticed her before or

realized what was going on around them, because when he first noticed her coming his way, his face showed surprise at seeing her. Then surprise turned into alarm and she saw him scan for an escape route.

He didn't move, though. Instead he stayed put and his stance changed as if he was ready and willing for a fight.

And while a hush had come over everyone nearby before, now there was total silence and unabashed staring.

When Addie reached the man she'd been about to marry, she said a simple, "Hello, Sean."

Both Sean and the pretty brunette beside him, who didn't seem to know how to react, muttered greetings.

Then the man who seemed almost frail to her now in comparison to Tanner said spitefully, "I suppose you want to talk…"

Addie shook her head. "I don't," she calmly assured him. "What you did, you did. As far as I'm concerned, it's water under the bridge."

"Really?" her former fiancé said facetiously, as if he didn't believe that.

"Really," she verified matter-of-factly. "I actually think it was for the best, so let's just go on from here. Bygones."

"Bygones?" Sean repeated with more sting in his huffy tone.

"I think we can do that, don't you?" Addie asked, her neutrality aided by seeing in him what she'd seen in rebellious children caught at something they had no defense for and posturing rather than admitting wrongdoing.

"Bygones…sure, why not," he said, putting his arm possessively around the wedding planner. "I got what I wanted."

"Don't be an ass, man," Tanner advised quietly from where he stood behind Addie, having trailed her without her even being aware of it.

Sean hugged the wedding planner closer, and his expression turned into a smirk.

Obviously he wasn't going to be gracious, but having offered him the olive branch Addie didn't feel there was anything else she needed to do.

So she merely said, "I only wish you well, Sean—"

"I'm doing very well, thanks," he answered in a playground sort of taunt.

Addie nodded. "I'm glad," she said.

Tanner bent over and whispered into her ear, "I'll knock his block off if you want…"

She shook her head, smiling slightly. "How about a beer instead?"

"You got it," he agreed, stepping up to her side and joining her in walking away.

"You're a jerk, Barkley," someone shouted at Sean from the crowd.

Neither Addie nor Tanner turned to see who it was. They just kept going until they were on the pathway that ran behind the booths.

They stopped at the booth devoted to his brother's

brewery. "I'm taking two of these," he informed Micah, who was working the counter-like front end.

"Sure," the older Camden brother called over his shoulder as Tanner picked two bottles of his brother's citrus-flavored beer from a case.

"Thanks," Tanner said before using the bottles he held in one hand by their necks to point to the area of the square where picnic tables were set up.

Addie chose the one farthest from where anyone was sitting, taking a few more deep breaths as she sat on the bench to ease the tension from her encounter with her ex.

Tanner untwisted the caps on both beers, gave her one, then lifted a long leg over the opposite bench to sit across the table from her. He took a swig of his beer but didn't say anything, giving her a minute.

It was a minute she needed and she appreciated that he was intuitive enough to recognize it.

Then she tasted her beer. "Oh, that's good!" she said. "I heard it was, but I hadn't tasted it. I actually thought it was a little weird to have fruity beer. But it really does work—this has a touch of tartness that I like."

Tanner nodded and took another gulp of his drink before he said, "So…"

Addie smiled. "Now you've met Sean…" she said in a singsong tone to lighten the reality of the encounter.

"That's the guy you were going to marry." Tanner said without any judgment in his voice.

"Well, sort of. What you just saw was something

I've never seen from him before and I'm not sure where that came from…guilt or embarrassment, maybe?"

"What have you seen from him before?"

"More…" she considered how to describe Sean's pursuit of her and decided on "puppy dog."

"I think that puppy caught rabies," Tanner muttered before he went on. "So you met him when he moved here and turned the jewelry store into an insurance office," Tanner said, repeating what she'd told him before. "And the puppy-dog thing—when did that start?"

"He asked me out five minutes into our first conversation. Later he said that for him it was love at first sight."

"But that wasn't what it was for you."

"I didn't *dis*like him, but there wasn't any kind of spark. In fact I turned him down for the date. I was busy with the start of the school year, so I really didn't have time, but I also hoped he'd get the hint that I wasn't really interested."

"But he didn't."

"No, he kept asking—"

"And you kept saying no?"

"I did. In fact I even introduced him to one of the other teachers at school, but that didn't work, either."

"Eventually he wore you down and sparks did fly?" Tanner asked.

Addie denied that with a shake of her head. "It was Della who talked me into going out with Sean after he'd been here awhile. She said I should get to know him. Kelly agreed—they both thought he was a nice guy. A nice *single* guy who was my age, cute, employed—"

"I know the drill—a fresh face in a small town is hard to come by," Tanner contributed. "If you haven't hit it off with any of the locals you've known your whole life, you shouldn't count out a newbie with qualifications until you've given them a shot."

"That was what they both said. I half thought he just wanted to sell me insurance and they were getting me into a sales call."

Tanner laughed. "Did he try to sell you insurance?"

"No, he only tried to sell me on him and giving him the opportunity to win me over. He said he knew he could and he wasn't going to stop until he did."

"That definitely has the ring of a salesman. But he must have been right if you were about to marry him. So for him it was love at first sight. What was it for you? Love at first date, or second date or third?"

Addie made a face. "No… I guess what I felt for Sean just sort of…inched in?"

Tanner chuckled. "You're asking me?"

"It's not like…" She wasn't sure how to succinctly say it, but for some reason she didn't want Tanner to believe what everyone else naturally had assumed. She finally settled on, "I didn't ever fall head over heels in love with Sean."

"Whoa, whoa, whoa," Tanner said. "You gave me grief because I've only been in take-'em or leave-'em relationships, and now you're telling me you were going to *marry* somebody *you* felt that way about?"

Addie made another face. "It wasn't that I could take him or leave him," she hedged. "I mean, okay, it was at the start. Della and Kelly were right—he was a nice guy, I liked him, we had a good time together. But—"

"He was strictly in the friend zone."

"Yeah. On my part that's all it was for...well, to be honest, for the two months we dated before things in my life started to crash. In fact, after seeing him for those two months I was looking for a way to bow out of dating him because I was afraid I might be leading him on and I didn't want to do that. Then Dad got sick and—"

"You thought it was okay to lead the guy on?" Tanner joked.

"No! I tried to cut Sean loose then, when I was about to move back home. We had the talk where I *told* him we were never going to be anything but friends. He just wouldn't accept it. He said that friends became more than friends all the time and he wasn't giving up on me. I thought he was just saving face, that when I moved back in with my parents, when I was too busy taking care of them and working and could never see him he'd find someone who *was* available and that would be that."

"But no?"

"I moved in with my folks and Sean started coming by for visits—he also had the excuse of being my parents' insurance agent—"

"That was handy," Tanner commented.

"He came in swearing he was just there as a friend, and what could I do? My parents thought it was so nice of him. He'd bring dinners, he kept my dad in beer and talked sports with him, he brought Mom the crossword puzzles she liked—"

"I'm betting they *loved* him."

"Oh, they did."

"But you saw that that wasn't all altruistic, right? He couldn't get to you through the front door, so he came in through the back," Tanner said with some caution.

"I did see what he was doing and I talked to him about it—I told him it wouldn't change anything. But he swore he was just there as a friend to the three of us."

"And was he only acting like a friend to you?"

"He was. For a long time—"

"Until he wasn't?"

"After more months of that than we'd dated, he did start to hang around after my parents went to bed so we were alone and—"

"And you didn't kick him out."

"I have to admit, I started to look forward to it because he'd become one of the few outlets I had from work and caregiving—"

"And there was the insurance salesman waiting in the wings..."

"What can I say? Time alone with Sean wasn't work, and he made sure to always keep everything light. An hour or two after Mom and Dad were asleep, sitting with Sean and watching some romantic comedy DVD he'd brought over, or just having him update me on the local gossip, or whatever—"

"Became an outlet," Tanner concluded for her.

"He even helped me with the funerals," she went on. "He helped Mom and Della and me through Dad's, then helped Della and me through Mom's... He just bent over backward to do whatever he could from the beginning of all that to the end of it."

"So when did it get more than just friendly?"

"When Dad died I did turn to Sean for comfort," she admitted. "Nothing big...he was just a shoulder to cry on, he took my arm here and there during the funeral—that sort of thing. It was after that, when I was on to caring only for Mom and Sean was still helping out that there was a second first kiss, a restart of the couple kind of things. Nothing pushy or aggressive, just...sweet..."

"I get the picture," Tanner assured her.

"And the longer that went on—the help, the support, the kindness, the understanding, the—"

"Puppy-dog adoration?"

"Yeah, that, too—but at that point there was some ego boost to having this guy still hanging around, to have that kind of devotion," she confessed. "And the longer it all went on, I did start to have..." Addie sighed. "I don't know... I suppose the best way to put it is that I started to have affection for Sean. Affection in a sort of loving way."

"Affection in a sort of loving way," Tanner repeated. "But still no sparks?"

"No," she answered in a near whisper, feeling some guilt. "But a sort of love," she reiterated.

"That's gratitude, Addie," Tanner pointed out. "Maybe deep gratitude, but still—"

"There's no question I was grateful to Sean. But by the time I'd lost both my parents it had started to feel like maybe there was more to it than that."

Although even as she defended herself, she knew that Tanner was shining a light on something she couldn't leave in the shadows any longer.

Was what she'd felt for Sean by the time her parents had passed what she'd thought it was? Or had it merely been appreciation of such magnitude—at a time when she was vulnerable—that it had seemed like more? That she'd convinced herself it was more?

Sean had done so much for her without ever being asked, and ultimately the truth was that she wasn't sure she would have made it through or been able to do what she'd done without his help.

So yes, she *had* been profoundly grateful to him.

"I *did* want to thank Sean, to repay him for everything he'd done..." she confided in Tanner. "When he asked me to move in with him after Mom died, when we had to sell the house to pay the medical bills...it didn't seem right to turn him down. It seemed like maybe I did owe him at least giving us a chance,"

"So when did you agree to marry him?"

"Three weeks before Della had Poppy and died— he proposed and with a lot of encouragement from Della, I said yes. We'd settled in pretty comfortably with each other. We had a lot in common. We didn't fight. We both saw ourselves staying in Merritt, married, with a family."

"I'm still not hearing that there were any sparks!"

"Not every relationship, not every marriage has them!" she countered. "Sean told me over and over how much he loved me. And I *did* have feelings for him—warm, comfortable feelings. It's the day-to-day that's important, that goes the distance, and we *were* good when it came to that. Sean had proved he would stick around through thick and thin—that's important, too. If other things weren't so exciting... well—"

"Wow, you talked yourself into a lot with this guy," Tanner said. "Or he talked you into a whole lot, I'm not sure which."

"Sean had already been in the trenches with me. I'd learned what a good team we made, how much it helped not to be alone through the rough times," Addie defended herself.

"Okay, I can see that," Tanner conceded. "But how did it go from all of that to *him* leaving *you* at the altar?"

"Well, the wedding planner," she said, pointing out the obvious.

But she also knew it wasn't only the other woman, and she decided to be honest, that Tanner might as well know the rest for his own sake.

"Even though Sean said he wanted to have kids, fatherhood didn't really fit him well," Addie told Tanner. "When Della died there was no question I was going to take Poppy, raise her. Sean said all the right things—that he wanted the three of us to be a family, that he wanted to help me raise her, to be a father to her. And I believed him. But when it came to the reality of having a baby around I started to see a different side to him."

"Did he help out with her the way he had with your folks?"

"He didn't help out at all. It was a complete turn-around from what he'd done with Mom and Dad. Granted, they were adults and Sean wasn't part of their hands-on care. But with Poppy, he was more like Della had been with Mom and Dad. Changing diapers made him gag. He couldn't stand the smell of the formula, so he wouldn't mix that or be any-where around when I did. He wouldn't feed her or burp her. He didn't want to hold her—again, if she spit up, he gagged. There was a lot of gagging..." Addie joked. "He said he just wasn't a baby person. But my mom always said my dad never changed a diaper or gave Della or me a bottle, so I thought maybe it was kind of a throwback to older genera-tions... and my dad ended up being a great father."

"But when it came down to actually signing on for the long haul of parenthood the guy ditched out."

Addie shrugged. "Or maybe Stephanie finally lit those sparks you keep talking about..."

Tanner shook his head in more disbelief. "The guy pulled out all the stops to have you—and he worked at it for a *long* time. I think he couldn't stand sharing you. He'd shared you with your folks, biding his time, knowing there would be an end to it. But when it came to a lifetime of sharing you with another man's kid..." He shook his head again, this time fatalistically, not putting the rest of the words to it.

He tossed their now-empty beer bottles into the nearby trash can as he said, "But if you weren't really into him or marrying him—"

"His leaving me at the altar saved me from myself," Addie finished, seeing what Tanner had shown her about misreading her feelings for Sean.

Tanner got to his feet and held out his hand to her. "Before meeting your ex I was enjoying myself—I forget what it's like here when I'm gone but tonight it all came back to me and I was thinking how glad I was to be here with you. Let's not end it on this. Give me one dance before we go."

Addie looked at the hand he was offering, inclined to accept it and imagining herself stepping out onto the dance floor with him. She couldn't think of a better way to get them both out of the doldrums of that conversation.

"But what about Sean—he could be there..." she reminded him.

Tanner smiled again, as if that possibility didn't faze him. "I think I can handle him. I *know* you can," he joked. "If he's still there that's his problem. Let it eat his heart out."

Addie wasn't interested in seeing her ex-fiancé again tonight. But dancing with Tanner? That was too enticing to pass up.

So she did exactly what she wanted to do and placed her hand in Tanner's.

He grinned and led her in the direction they'd come from.

When they reached the makeshift dance floor there was no sign of Sean or the wedding planner.

Tanner swung Addie to face him with enough force that she landed right up against him, catching her around the waist and bringing their clasped hands to sandwich between them for a slow dance.

They'd done a lot of talking and now dancing was the only thing they did.

The music, the movement, being in Tanner's arms, was cathartic. It allowed Addie to let go of everything she'd been feeling and remembering and thinking since confronting her ex. It allowed her to let go of the stress that had come with it. And oddly, in the course of that it also allowed some of the stress and frustration she'd been carrying around since Wednesday night to dissolve.

Leaving only that craving for Tanner she hadn't been able to shake. The craving without the arguments against them. Without even the concerns.

And what that left was instinct alone, telling her with certainty that Kelly was right to encourage her to just suspend all the shouldn'ts and giving in to the longing that nothing had been able to contain. That just for now she could—she needed to—merely give in to what she wanted.

And what she wanted was one night of ignoring all reason to have the man she was dancing with…

The slow song finished and a livelier tune followed it, but for a moment Tanner kept her where she was.

"Home? Or do you want to stay here and shake it up?" he asked.

"Home," Addie answered without having to think about it anymore.

Tanner let go of her waist but retained her hand now that he had it, tucking his elbow into hers to keep it in his possession. Then they headed away from the town square and began the short walk to her house.

"I barely made it through last night," he informed her along the way.

"Were you sick? I wondered why you brought Poppy's bottle and then just left the nursery..." And the possibility that he hadn't been ill was better than thinking the other things she'd thought—among them that he was distancing himself to let her know ending things Wednesday night had been ending things for good...

"I wasn't sick. I was doing my damnedest to stay away from you."

"Oh..." she said, unsure what that might mean.

"It seemed like that was what you'd decided was best."

"Did it?" she asked.

"It did. And that's okay...it was your call. But tonight, if you're making the same call and since there's no baby to feed, I'm gonna leave you at your door and go out to the farm."

It wasn't a threat. It was simple information.

"And if I make a different call…then what?" she asked.

"Then I'll answer that one," he promised, his voice full of innuendo, and his hand squeezing hers.

They reached her house and went up onto the porch. In a motion less forceful but much like the one that had started their dance, he spun her to face him again. Leaving more distance between them this time, though.

The porch light was on. The street was well lit. The moon was high. And Addie could see every detail of his face when she looked up into it. That face so finely chiseled it was almost too handsome to be real.

"*Are* you making a different call tonight?" he asked.

"You're really playing it safe, aren't you?"

"Yes, ma'am. I won't even kiss you good-night."

That *did* sound like a threat. Or maybe it did because him kissing her was on her mind yet again and she didn't like that he might not do it.

"So what'll it be? A handshake and a good-night and I'll take off now?"

She knew that was what he would do if she told him to.

And she knew how sorry she'd be if he did…

"I don't want you to go to the farm," she said.

His smile was sexy again as he leaned down and kissed her a choirboy's kiss that didn't last. "Where then?"

She shook her head to chastise him for trying to get her to say it out loud. Then she opened her unlocked front door and went inside, bringing him with her by their clasped hands and closing the door behind them.

And if that wasn't invitation enough, when she faced him again she went straight for the top button of his shirt and undid it.

"Uh-uh," he said, covering her hands with one of his to stop them before they could move on to the next. "Slow and easy…" His free hand rose to the side of her face, tipping it so he could peer into her eyes, an intensity equal to those unique blue ones of his. "I have never wanted anything more than I want you and I'm taking my time."

There was something about the way he said that, the raw emotion in his voice, that told her it was true. And left her thinking he had the right to that same honesty.

"Then we're even," she confessed quietly. "Because I can't remember ever wanting anything more than I want you."

She saw a smile from him then that she hadn't seen before—a smile that made her believe she was seeing the man inside, completely unveiled.

He kissed her a second time, this one also unhurried but with nothing chaste about it, and now that he'd set a more moderate pace she concentrated on relishing this that she'd fantasized about, imagined, pined for…

His lips parted and coaxed hers apart, too, so

his tongue could take the kiss to another level. Another level where he was so adept that that alone doubled her arousal as it made her think of what was to come.

Since he'd made her leave his shirt buttoned she raised both hands to his shoulders, to his back, and tested the feel of that expanse in the cool slipperiness of cotton rather than knit, deciding that she didn't like it, as well. The knit of the fitted T-shirts he ordinarily wore mimicked the real thing better. And it was the real thing she just had to have her hands on. So she tugged the shirt from his waistband and snaked underneath to his warm smooth skin.

Her tongue fenced with his as her hands memorized the texture and terrain of his strong back. But as nice as that all was, as much as she was enjoying it, as much as she understood the inclination to not rush, she just had to have more of him.

She drew her hands to his sides, she let her forearms finesse the rest of his shirttails free, and she kicked off the sandals she'd worn tonight.

The lack of shoes dropped her by two inches but Tanner didn't let there be a gap—he leaned farther forward as his hands went to her shoulders and kept her to that kiss that was growing ever more tantalizing.

Too tantalizing to go on in the entryway.

Addie retrieved her hands from under his shirt, ended that kiss, and recaptured the hand that had held hers all the way home so she could lead him up the steps to her room.

"You haven't changed your mind…" he teased but tested, too.

"I haven't," she told him without uncertainty. Then, over her shoulder she said, "So if you have, too bad!"

He laughed. "Nah…do with me what you will."

They reached her room and once she'd shut yet another door behind them, Tanner spun her a third time to restart their kiss with a new, unleashed hunger that made it demanding now. And he didn't hesitate to unfasten the buttons that closed the straps of her dress so that it drifted to her ankles before those big hands splayed against her back.

Ah, so now it was okay to do some undressing…

Glad that she hadn't bypassed the lacy demi-cup bra and matching black lace bikinis from the honeymoon suitcase, she still wasn't going to be the only one of them exposed, so she sent her hands back to the mission he'd cut short before.

This time Tanner didn't keep her from unbuttoning his shirt. And he had no complaint when her hands glided inside the gapping front to rock-solid abs.

Rock-solid abs that led her to his belt buckle.

But even as she set that and his waistband free it occurred to her that while she might have had a fair share of the sight of that torso cast in knit—and even in the tank top undershirts he wore to bed— she now had the chance to see it bare…

The mere thought of that turned her on all the more, and that added some heat to the kiss that was already openmouthed and unrestrained as she finessed his shirt from his shoulders.

He accommodated her so that it ended up on the floor around their feet, too. Then he made her forget that she'd intended to get a gander of him when he wrapped only one arm around her and captured her breast in his other hand.

That felt so good and set so much alive in her that it almost seemed unfair. Her nipple tightened enough to escape the top edge of her bra and nestled into his palm almost all on its own.

His hand closed firmly around her, kneading that globe of flesh and stealing her breath with the pure pleasure of it. And when that wasn't enough, he freed her breast completely and made it even better.

But she'd had a goal of her own...to see him.

Only now it wasn't merely his upper half she wanted in that picture...

Whether it was that idea or the gentle pinch of her nipple—or both—a tingle went through her that made her determined, and she returned to that dangling belt buckle, to those unhooked trousers, discovering that there was so much of him contained inside that his zipper was already partially lowered.

Emboldened by the effect she was having on him, she opened the zipper the rest of the way.

But before she did some setting free of her own, there was a rumble in Tanner's throat and he abruptly ended the kiss, deserting her breast, too.

From under her half-mast eyelids Addie watched

as he put his hand into his pants pocket and pulled out a condom.

"I didn't want to be unprepared…just in case…" he said with another, much more gravelly laugh, tossing it to the bed behind her before he dropped those slacks and whatever was under them and kicked them away.

And Addie finally got her look at a body even more magnificent than she'd anticipated.

He didn't seem to notice that she was devouring the sight of him as he bent just enough to kiss her shoulder while he made quick work of unhooking her bra. And she was so enraptured by the sight of him that she was only vaguely aware of the slightly cooler air that came to her own bare breasts when her bra disappeared, too.

Then he growled slightly and swept her up into his arms, taking her to the bed where he gently tossed her onto the mattress before a slight leap brought him there with her.

All bets were off then.

His mouth went to her naked breasts, first one and then the other—his teeth, his tongue, doing things to her that were wild and abandoned, arousing in her a raging excitement that very nearly swept her away.

And just as she was trying not to let that happen, he reached down and took off her bikinis and sent his hand on a straight path that ended between her thighs.

She didn't intend to moan but couldn't help it any

more than she could help writhing just a bit under the double whammy he was giving as her fingers dug into his back.

Eager to touch him as intimately as he was touching her, she did some of her own exploring of that long, hard staff.

His groan came from deep in his throat and his hips angled in her direction as if her hand were a magnetic force that iron shaft couldn't repel. And unless she was mistaken, it grew even harder in her grip.

In a flash Tanner was gone, leaving only a brush of chilly air in his wake. Then he was back again, protection in place as the front of his glorious body ran the length of her side and his mouth did a fervent revisit to her breast as his massive thigh insinuated itself between hers and rose to the juncture of her legs.

Legs she willingly opened to him and that honed thigh that had talents of its own pressed up tight against her.

Then his mouth left her breast so he could reposition himself completely over her, kissing her with another carnal kiss while he came into her so slowly, so sublimely, that Addie arched up to aid the cause and accommodate the full length and girth of him.

Then the kiss became an act of love all in itself as he pulsed inside of her, flexing that other impressive muscle of his, delving just a little deeper into that sanctuary, backing out just a little, then diving in again...

Slow and easy—the way it had all begun—Addie could cherish every inch out and yearn for every inch back in. And out again. And in.

She kept up with the tempo when it increased and increased and increased until suddenly she was on a ride that took her over so completely she could only hang on. Higher and higher it kept climbing until she reached a blinding peak that exploded inside her, overwhelmed her, and shocked her with an intensity she hadn't known was possible.

Her legs wrapped around his, pulling him in deeper still where he erupted in a climax that melded their bodies at their core and held them there as wave after wave washed over them both and swept them away.

Away to the other side of that pinnacle where the descent left them wilted, depleted, satiated...

He let some of his weight rest on her then and buried his face in the top of her head. "I think you ruined me."

"I hurt you?" she asked, alarmed, afraid she'd been too carried away.

But Tanner just groaned pleasurably once more and pushed his hips into her. "You ruined me for anything that comes after this—the best food, the best booze, parachuting out of a plane...what could ever equal it, let alone top it?"

Addie smiled and kissed his broad shoulder, keeping her own utter amazement to herself despite also being thrilled that she hadn't disappointed him.

Neither of them said anything for a while, just

lying there, their bodies perfectly one, until Tanner said, "Let me take care of things...don't go anywhere."

He slid out of her, rolled, and was gone into her bathroom. But only for a moment before he came back, dropped onto the mattress beside her as if he barely had the strength to do that and scooped her to lie beside him so tightly her leg had nowhere to go but over his.

"We need to do that again to believe it," he announced.

"Right now?" she goaded as her head found the hollow of his shoulder.

He laughed again. "Give me a minute. Thinking about this kept me up all night last night, remember?"

He turned his head to kiss the top of hers and stayed there, his breath warm. "But that really was something." he whispered, awe in his voice again.

"For me, too," Addie whispered in return.

Her cheek was blissfully resting on his chest and she felt him give in to exhaustion just when that was overtaking her, as well. So she closed her eyes and just absorbed the incredible feeling of their naked bodies together, his arms locked around her as if he didn't want her to get away.

And as sleep came for her Addie was still marveling at what they'd just shared.

And wondering how anything could go back to normal.

Chapter Eight

There was nothing like an early Saturday morning in Merritt. For Tanner there was nothing like that particular early Saturday morning.

It was barely seven o'clock when he decided to do what he knew his grandfather was doing at that same time out at the farm—he took his coffee onto the front porch.

Unlike the Camden family's porch—or even Micah's—the porch on Addie's dilapidated old house needed work and had no furniture at all. So Tanner sat on the top step and planted his bare feet flat on the cracked walkway that came up to the house from the sidewalk.

Wearing only a white T-shirt and a pair of gray sweatpants, he braced his elbows on his widespread knees and cupped his mug between both hands, staring out at the neighborhood around him.

He could hear the faint hum of a lawnmower from the other end of the block. The scent of fresh-cut grass mingled with the farther-off smell of manure coming in from the farms just outside of town. And the sense of calm, of peace, of contentment, was almost palpable to him.

Years ago, when he'd been an eighteen-year-old champing at the bit to get out of the small town, to go to Annapolis, to become a marine, he'd had no appreciation for what seemed to him at that moment like a little pocket of paradise.

Why hadn't it seemed like that to him before?

Growing up here, small-town life was all he'd known, and he guessed he'd taken it for granted. So maybe there was no surprise that it hadn't seemed like anything special to him. But that didn't explain why he hadn't felt this same way about being here in the years since, when he'd seen so much worse beyond this small haven.

Yes, on the few other occasions when he'd been back to Merritt he'd felt a sense of pride that his being a marine helped to preserve and maintain what was here. For his grandfather. For old friends. For teachers and acquaintances like Gloria. For everyone who wanted to be here.

But this was the first time he was glad Merritt and this lifestyle were still here for him, too. The first time he was having this sense that it *was* here for him, too.

Here for the taking.

There'd been something different going on this trip—and not just the situation with Poppy and Addie. Until this morning he'd been only vaguely aware of how he was feeling, but *because* of the situation with Poppy and Addie he hadn't put much thought into it.

Now, sitting there soaking in that early Saturday morning and liking it as much as he was, he had to wonder about what was different this time…

The answer wasn't pretty. Because the reason he felt differently about being in Merritt now was that Della was gone.

Even if his own experiences with her were complex, he was still sorry that she'd ended up having such a short life. He was honestly sorry that she had died. He'd seen Addie's grief and he was sorry for that, too. Sorry that Poppy would never know the woman who had given birth to her, sorry that Della would not see her daughter grow up. There was nothing that wasn't sad about it, about a life lost so young.

But to himself alone he admitted that being in Merritt without any possibility of encountering Della, without feeling the ever-present need to brace for something she might come at him with, was like being here in an entirely different way.

A less restricted way, where he didn't always need to be alert or cautious. A way that made him feel as if he could genuinely relax, settle in, let the comforts and pleasures and benefits and rewards of this place sink in.

He could just be home for the first time in seventeen years. Even if he wasn't at the farm but was here in this ramshackle old place. With a baby that might be his and all the complications that could bring.

Then there was Addie. Despite the fact that she was one of the complications, there was nothing about her that *felt* like a complication. There was nothing about her that made him feel bad at all…

She was upstairs asleep.

Sleep wasn't something they'd had more than a couple of scattered hours of last night. Or this morning when they'd showered together at dawn and then answered another call of the bed after that.

But when she'd dozed off afterward, his years of early risings had kicked in and kept him awake. So he'd left her to rest and come downstairs for some refueling in the form of strong black coffee.

To refuel and to force himself to keep his hands off her for a while so she *could* rest.

Where did you come from? he silently asked of her.

And how could she have been right under his nose without him seeing her until now? Without him knowing just how amazing she was?

His grandfather's reaction that morning almost a week ago when he'd told Ben about the arrangement he'd made with Addie, and his grandfather's warning against doing anything to hurt her made complete sense now.

Addie truly was exceptional. She was kind and generous and fair. She was loving. Caring. She was brave. And she still managed to be fun. And funny. And plucky enough to make him smile just thinking about her.

And she was so damn sexy.

She was more to him than he'd ever thought anyone could be...

He took a drink of his coffee, wondering if lack of sleep was putting strange things in his head. Because no one got to him like that. He didn't *let* anyone get to him like that.

But when he pictured Addie upstairs in that room, that bed where they'd spent the last hours, when he considered just how much he was itching to go back up there to her, when he thought about spending today with her, tonight, tomorrow...

There wasn't anything else that appealed to him. There wasn't anything he wanted more.

He took another drink of coffee, then took a deep breath of the fresh country air. He told himself to get some control. But none of it changed anything. Addie was still first and foremost in every thought, every image.

It occurred to him that that had been the case for a while now. For several days she'd been the first thing on his mind the instant he woke up in the morning.

And she was the last thing he thought about when he drifted to sleep at night.

He didn't know how or when it had started, but somehow these feelings had crept up on him. Even before making love to her last night, she'd started to mean a great deal to him.

And now here he was, wanting a whole lot of nights with her like last night. And a whole lot of Saturday mornings like this one…

He took yet another swig of coffee. *Maybe last night knocked some screws loose in you,* he said to himself.

There was no denying, spending the night with Addie had been pretty powerful. But was the best sex of his life enough to change things—change him—that drastically?

Rules. You have rules, man.

Women never come first, the Marines come first, he reminded himself.

The rules dictated that. He'd made the rules. He followed the rules.

The rules also dictated the kind of women he would be with—women who were nothing like Della.

And Addie is Della's freaking sister!

That internal voice shouting at him forced Tanner to think about the time he met Addie again after all these years. His first impression—*before* she'd started to get to him.

She'd run through emotions at lightning speed— she'd been suspicious of him, riled up, defensive, accusatory, afraid, outraged. Tears had come into those big beautiful brown eyes of hers. She'd tried bargaining with him, scaring him off—and that had been in the space of half an hour. So there was no question that she'd been excessively emotional, though he'd certainly given her plenty of reason to react that way. Still, one of the rules was avoiding women who showed excessive emotion.

There had also been the day they'd cleaned Gloria's yard. Addie had been quiet, impatient, out of sorts.

All of that was Della-like, too.

Although if it had been Della, that bad mood that Addie had called prickliness would have escalated. And escalated and escalated—into tears and accusations and drama.

But Addie had admitted she was prickly, *de*-escalated, and promised it wouldn't happen again. And it hadn't.

That was about as *un*-Della-like as it could have been.

And like their first meeting, that day at Gloria's Addie's heightened show of emotions had good reason. What could be better reasons than the possibility of her losing the baby she loved or being left to clean up after a wedding where she'd been left at the altar? Who *wouldn't* have been running on high-octane emotions in those situations?

And since then?

There had been times when she'd had a cooler head than he had—like when Poppy had been on that crying jag. Not only hadn't it ruffled Addie, she'd managed *his* overreaction!

She'd been right when she'd whittled down his history and pinpointed that the only relationships he'd gotten into had been with women a lot like him. Women who put things other than him first. Women who weren't any more invested in their relationships than he'd been. Women with one foot out the door, too.

Women he could take or leave.

But now, comparing even this brief time with Addie to what had constituted long-term relationships for him, he realized none of those other relationships *could* compare.

None of them had drawn him in the way a night just sitting on the floor talking to Addie had. Or opened his eyes to things about himself the way talking to Addie had, the way she'd opened his eyes to the damage Della had done when he'd only believed she'd taught him a lesson.

And when it came to the sex?

He wasn't *in*experienced in that area of his life. And he'd never had another night like last night. There had been *emotion* for him in that, too. It hadn't only been physical and that was an all-new experience he didn't quite understand.

Maybe it was because there *was* so much more of a connection with Addie than he'd ever had with anyone else. Because yes, he *did* feel a connection with her.

Even as he admitted that to himself he did it with the caution of approaching a loaded bomb.

But it was true. He felt a connection to Addie.

A connection that included Poppy...

That realization creeped up on him but when he thought about it, it struck him that somewhere in learning to care for the baby, Poppy had become something more to him, too...

Despite being wary of dropping his guard in case the DNA results proved he wasn't her father, that tiny bundle had slipped in under the radar and gotten to him in the same way Addie had.

She wasn't just the potential for his life to be turned upside down. She wasn't just a training tool. She was a warm little bundle who looked up at him with pure trust, searching his face with wonder and fascination. She was warm little bundle who cuddled against him, and made a tiny nothing-of-a-sound that was the sweetest thing he'd ever heard. She was a warm little bundle that—when he held her and it was actually going well for them both—made him feel a kind of peace, a sense that all could be right in the world, that was another thing he'd never felt before.

And yes, he cared about her. Cared about the kind of life she would have. Cared that nothing bad ever happened to her. Cared that she was always safe and secure, loved...

Lost in his thoughts, Tanner's gaze had gone to the ground. For no reason, he raised it then and it landed on the dilapidated mailbox at the curbside sidewalk. The mailbox had lost its back end so he could see into it from the porch and there was something inside that must have been delivered the day before.

Tanner got up and went out to retrieve it.

But the manilla envelope wasn't addressed to Addie. His name was on it.

Everything went on hold for Tanner at that moment when he recalled that he'd given the hospital lab his cell number but this address as where he was staying until the results of the DNA test came in.

And there in Tanner's hands was the information that would tell him if he was a father or not.

Tanner looked at the envelope and he just knew.

He might not have had any intuition about whether or not Poppy was his at the start of this, when his brother had asked him, but looking at that envelope now, he knew.

Still, he opened it and took a sheet of paper out only far enough to read the results.

A positive match for paternity.

For a minute Tanner didn't hear the mower at the end of the block.

For a minute he didn't breathe in the country air.

For a minute he just stared at those words on the page.

Until once again Addie was his first thought.

Addie and how much this could hurt her.

How much *he* could hurt her...

Oh, Big Ben, what'd I do...he mentally asked his grandfather. *And how the hell am I gonna fix it?*

There was one solution staring Tanner in the face.

He could choose to walk away, leave Addie to be Poppy's guardian, to adopt her, the way she wanted, the way she'd planned.

If he took all financial responsibility so Addie didn't have that burden, if he kept some kind of contact, if he visited or checked in, that would be a semblance of doing the right thing without hurting Addie.

And that way she wouldn't have to take yet another hit. In fact, he could make sure that his being Poppy's father only helped her.

And Addie would have what she'd already made clear repeatedly that she wanted—to be Poppy's mother, to raise her, to make sure she kept close the only family she had left.

Although the minute his grandfather discovered he had a great-granddaughter, Tanner knew Addie's family would extend. The old man would embrace another generation of Camdens and Addie along with it. Addie whom Ben already admired and respected and wanted to protect just as an acquaintance. If she became the mother of his great-granddaughter there was no way Ben wouldn't make Addie as much a part of the Camden family as Poppy was. So again, Addie would be in better shape.

And I could just go on... Tanner thought.

It was a way to make sure he didn't cause Addie any more pain than she'd already suffered in the last year and a half.

It was the best thing he could do for Poppy: Addie was the best gift he could give her.

His grandfather would be thrilled.

And I'll just go on...he thought for the second time.

Then why did the idea make him so damn mad? And so damn jealous?

Doubly jealous when he added to the future picture forming in his head and imagined Addie meeting someone who wasn't a jerk who'd leave her at the altar. When he added the picture of Addie getting married, making that someone else Poppy's dad, having more kids with that man... And having nights like last night with that man...

All of it here, in Merritt...

Tanner's teeth were clenched hard and he really was seeing red.

If that image of the future wasn't the ultimate punishment for one drunken, weak moment eleven and half months ago, he didn't know what was.

He did know—all of a sudden and with certainty—that he couldn't do it.

Plain and simple. Plain and simple and despite training that had broken him away from this kind of life to rebuild him into a marine, and despite the life he'd lived for seventeen years.

Despite training to *not* put himself or his own needs or desires ahead of honor, of integrity. Ahead of his duties, his obligations. Ahead of doing the right thing.

But when it came to Addie, he just couldn't.

Because what he felt for her was more than a *connection* and he finally admitted it.

He'd fallen for her. Completely. Hard. Head over heels. He was in love with her.

And under no circumstances could he step aside and let everything he'd just played out in his head happen without him.

Under no circumstances could anyone but him be here for Addie.

And under no circumstances could anyone but him share in taking care of Poppy, either. No matter how unskilled he was at it. It was still his face she looked up at now that made her smile, and he wasn't giving that up for anything.

He didn't want to just be her dad on paper. He wanted to be her dad.

He picked up his cup and flung the remaining coffee, which had gone cold, onto the weeds that needed to be dealt with, like so many other things around here. He realized he also didn't want to let someone else deal with those things or turn this damn old house into a nice place to live.

So he was in love with Addie, he thought.

He wanted to be a dad to this child he'd brought into the world.

And it felt good to be home in Merritt again.

What was he going to do about all that?

But he knew.

For the second time this morning, he just knew.

Chapter Nine

"Oh...you smell so good..." Addie said without even opening her eyes, waking to the feel of Tanner gently stroking her cheek.

The sun had just been rising when she'd closed her eyes but now she could feel the warmth of it coming in through the open curtains, so she knew she'd been asleep for a little while.

A little while was enough if Tanner was waking her for another round of what had occupied them since coming back from the Summer Kick-Off Festival...

"I want you to come downstairs," he said quietly. And more seriously than she'd ever heard him before.

Addie opened her eyes.

He was sitting next to her on the edge of the bed, still gorgeous in the light of day. He was clean-shaven, his hair washed but obviously left to dry in disarray, and dressed in gray sweatpants and one of those tight, tight T-shirts again—one that, after the time they'd spent together, she could now feel free to take off him the way she'd been fantasizing about...

Except that his expression was serious, too, so she restrained herself. "Downstairs?" she echoed, her tone suggestive.

"I made coffee and I need to talk to you."

Talk...

That had nothing suggestive to it. It didn't sound good, sobering her considerably.

Was he going to warn her that this had been a one-night stand and since the night was over, so was this?

Addie closed her eyes again and did a mental reset.

It wasn't anything else for you, remember? she reminded herself. *It was just a way to get wanting him out of your system.*

So much for that! Their one night together only made her want him more.

Maybe the man was addictive, but she couldn't let that habit take hold.

And to make sure she didn't, she released everything she'd compartmentalized earlier—her resentment of his cold reaction to her sister seventeen years ago and the disillusionment she'd felt watching it, her fears of him taking Poppy, the worries about what kind of a father he would be to Poppy… She let it all flood through her again so she could hang onto the reality of what Tanner being here meant. So she could battle him.

When she opened her eyes, there was nothing of the Addie of the previous night left.

Maybe Tanner saw that because he took his hand away from her cheek.

"Looks like you had a second shower. I need a few minutes for another one, too. Alone…" she said, so clipped, so practical, so clearly ready to accept the edict that what happened last night was over and done with, that it made Tanner frown.

"Sure," he said as if he wasn't certain what was going on.

"Could you leave so I can get up?" Because she was naked under the sheet. And while modesty before this had been long gone, she was back to feeling the need for control, the need to not be too exposed.

"I'll be downstairs," he said, his own voice suddenly self-protective, too.

Addie had no idea why tears welled up in her eyes the minute he was gone, but she fought them.

She fought them through her quick shower and shampoo. She fought them as she dried off, brushed out her hair and put on not-from-the-honeymoon-suitcase bra and bikinis, a pair of black yoga pants and a serviceable white V-neck T-shirt with no sex appeal at all.

Slipping her feet into a pair of flip-flops and taking a few deep breaths to make sure those stupid tears were nowhere near the surface, she went downstairs, too.

Tanner was in the kitchen, leaning with his hips against the sink, his muscular arms crossed over the honed abs of a midsection that she'd repeatedly reveled in through the night and early-morning hours.

Only after the initial sight of him distracted her the way it always did, did she notice a manila envelope in the middle of the old, scarred kitchen table.

Tanner's gaze had gone to the same thing. "DNA results," he announced even though she hadn't asked.

Addie's heart sank.

Not only is he going to tell me last night was a one-time thing, he's going to tell me he's taking Poppy, too...

And it would likely be in that stilted, impervious way he'd been seventeen years ago...

Instantly the best night of her life turned into the worst morning of it. And after three deaths and being left at the altar, there were a slew of bad mornings in the competition.

Addie didn't say anything, buying herself every possible moment before this began.

But even without encouragement Tanner said, "I'm Poppy's father."

The lump in Addie's throat was so big she couldn't swallow, she couldn't even cry. She definitely couldn't speak.

But she didn't have to because Tanner was doing the talking.

"I'm telling you up front that I'm not taking her away from you."

"You'll leave her with me?" she said disbelievingly.

"I will," he answered.

But it seemed clear there was more to come. And he *had* said he was telling her this up front—that meant there was definitely more to come, didn't it? Another shoe to drop, maybe?

Addie waited for it.

"She's yours, Addie," Tanner said as if there was no question about it. "She's mine, too, but right now she's more yours than mine."

Right now?

"I'll do whatever has to be done to clear the way for you to adopt her," Tanner went on. "Whether that's me just signing off on you being her co-parent or even giving up my rights—we'll talk to a lawyer and make you formally, legally, her mom."

There had to be a catch…

"Since she *is* mine," Tanner was saying, "I'll support her, I'll pay for everything—child support and everything she needs over that, everything you need *because* of her. And you can call the shots on what kind of a relationship I have with her."

Maybe this was his ticket out after last night…

"Okay?" he said.

"Okay," Addie responded tentatively, not trusting this.

"That's how it is—how it will be—no matter what

comes of the rest of this. You're Poppy's mom—done deal, not an issue."

No matter what comes of the rest of this...

So there was definitely more to come.

She said another tentative "Okay."

"But..."

Addie stiffened up, bracing herself.

"But I don't want it to be just the two of you," he said, and this time that faint glimmer of vulnerability that she'd seen in him before sounded faintly in his voice. "This morning some things hit me kind of hard—"

"Seeing the DNA results in black-and-white?" Addie guessed.

"Actually, no. Once I decided that I couldn't take Poppy away from you—or you away from Poppy—what hit me was what *I* was giving up."

Another thought struck Addie to add to her unease. She wondered if this was the launch of some kind of guilt trip, if he was going to try to convince her *not* to accept his offer because he didn't want to be the bad guy in this. If he was going to try to make her feel as if she was doing something wrong by keeping his child from him—the child Della would undoubtedly have wanted him to have...

Then Tanner went on to tell Addie about his thought process, about the picturesque future he'd envisioned giving her and the baby.

"But I couldn't stand that I wasn't in that picture," he confessed.

"So you *do* want Poppy," Addie blurted out because she couldn't stand the suspense.

"I want you. And the baby that comes with you that also happens to be mine."

Of all the things Addie had thought were about to come at her, that wasn't one of them. It wasn't what she'd prepared herself for and it disarmed her to such a degree she had to shift gears...

So he *wasn't* telling her that last night had been a one-time thing?

He *was* telling her that he was Poppy's father, but he was also telling her that he wouldn't take Poppy away?

He was telling her that he wanted her, that he wanted Poppy, that he wanted to be a part of the picture...

And he was telling her all of it openly? Honestly? Unguardedly?

Early on she'd realized that fear was making her scattered; it was the reason she'd boxed it up. Now that it had been let loose, she was even more scattered, and though she tried to sort through what he was saying, she was still not convinced she was getting it right.

"I'm not sure I understand," she muttered.

Tanner pushed off the edge of the sink and crossed to her, taking both of her hands in his, looking from one of them to the other before he pulled them to his chest.

"I know this is coming at you like greased lightning, but that's kind of how it came at me this morning, too. I'm in love with you, Addie—and that's not something I've ever said to anyone else, because it isn't something I've ever felt for anyone else. It's why I could never hurt you by taking away Poppy. It's why instead of feeling any satisfaction in making sure you can have the future you want, it crushed me to think of you having that future without me in it. I want you to marry me. I want you and me to both be Poppy's parents. I want us to be a family—"

"That's what Sean said," she blurted out in pure reflex.

"*That's* not music to my ears…" Tanner said under his breath. "But I'm not that other guy." His grip around her hands tightened a bit to emphasize it.

"No, you're my sister's—"

"History," he interjected, cutting her off before she could put more words out there. "Our pasts are over and done with. Yours is and so is mine. What you and I have now, what's between us, is so far beyond that…"

Addie admitted there was no way in which she saw Tanner and her late sister in the same context anymore. That as she'd come to know Tanner on her own terms his past *had* faded. That as their own relationship had evolved, it had become genuinely their own relationship, outside of anything to do with her sister, even outside of Poppy.

And Sean was history for her, as well.

"Still, this is a lot…a giant leap," she observed. "Are you sure this isn't just…convenient?"

He laughed.

"I mean it—you didn't have the heart to take Poppy away from me, but now you know you're her father and you need help with that. Is this just what you came up with as a sensible solution all the way around?"

He smiled kindly. "Why? Because that's pretty much what brought you to accepting the other guy's proposal—being *sensible*?"

"That makes me the poster child for why it's a bad idea," she cautioned.

"Yeah, I was kind of blown away by all that *sensible* last night," he said sarcastically. "No, this isn't the *sensible* solution. And I couldn't stand it if it was that for you, either—that's why you being Poppy's mom isn't a question, so I can know that if you say yes to me, it isn't what it was when you said yes to the other guy."

If she said yes...

She looked up into Tanner's face, into his blue eyes. She thought about how he'd been there for her even before there had been anything at all going on between them—cleaning Gloria's yard, helping with the house, returning the wedding gifts. She thought about the support he'd silently given. The work he'd done.

She thought about the hours of talking to him about her parents, Della, Sean. About what a good listener he'd been, a good sounding board. About how—*because* he hadn't tiptoed around any of it, and *because* he hadn't been overly solicitous—it had been cathartic for her, strengthening.

She remembered how he'd approached the possibility that Poppy was his—stoically, honorably.

He'd absorbed what she'd thrown at him over Poppy—her ups and downs, her attempts to make him fail as a caregiver, her unsubtle discouragements. He'd been calm, reasonable, unshakable in his resolves.

She thought about the night they'd spent together, and the undeniable sparks that had flown...

And she began to see just what a good man he was, and how, out of his being a good man, more *had* grown between them than was ever in her relationship with Sean.

Looking up into that sculpted face she also began to realize that the distant, detached, reserved person she'd seen that afternoon seventeen years ago wasn't what he was presenting to her now.

Yes, she might have seen indications of it earlier, but as they'd grown closer that shell had dropped away. That even though there was still some reserve with Poppy, there was less of it as he became more comfortable with her. She knew now that what was beneath the veneer of the marine was a kind, caring man who had learned a harsh lesson at her sister's hands to be self-protective. But that self-protection was gone or he wouldn't be standing there saying he loved her. He wouldn't have let her see the vulnerable side of him. And with that two and two put together, she didn't have any doubt that he would ultimately be a loving father.

And husband. *Husband?*

They weren't seriously talking about that, were they? The dust was barely settled on her canceled wedding.

"It's so soon after Sean..." she heard herself say in response to her own wandering thoughts.

Tanner placed her hands on his shoulders and clasped his around her waist. "Yeah, it is," he agreed quietly, his voice a bit ragged. "And if all I am to you is a handyman and a night of great sex," he said as if there was a portion of him that was worried about that, "it'll kill me."

If all he was to her was a handyman and a night of great sex...

If all he was to her *was* only a rebound—that was what he was saying...

Addie's initial response to that was a humorless laugh because he was so much more than a handyman or great sex or a rebound.

But still, she told herself she had to think about it. That she had to know that she wasn't doing anything for the wrong reasons this time.

Because after all, she *was* on the rebound in a big way. She'd been left at that altar. Dumped unceremoniously for the entire town to see. The entire town felt sorry for her. Tanner would be a wickedly delicious comeback.

And Tanner had been right that she'd talked herself into a whole lot when it came to Sean. That she'd been more grateful to him than anything—what if *she* was the one of them opting for a clean fix? A way of emerging from that embarrassment in victory? A way of securely ensuring that she didn't lose Poppy to Poppy's rightful parent?

But when she looked deep inside herself she knew better. She'd been trying to put *him* in the category of someone she could take or leave.

She'd tried, but she hadn't achieved it, or it wouldn't have nearly shattered her a little while ago when she'd been afraid he was going to tell her she was a one and done.

No, she couldn't just take this man or leave him.

And she didn't have to look too deep to know that she'd fallen in love with him, too.

"You're a long way from just being a handyman and a night of great sex," she finally said. "But because you're a long way from it, I don't know if I can do the military-wife thing."

Tanner shook his head. "That was another part of this morning's shocks—" he said, going on to tell her how he'd discovered he wanted to be here in Merritt with her. Which he seemed to have thought out. "My degree is in cyber operations—that's technology, computers, security. It isn't what I ended up doing in the corps, but now I can use it either in the private sector or maybe work as a civilian for the military. I'm a commissioned officer—that means that I have a contract, that I can resign when my current contract is up and that's in a few weeks. I told you, I want to be in that picture of you and Poppy, and I want that picture taken here in Merritt."

"You're sure about that?"

"Not a question in my mind," he said without hesitation.

She searched his handsome face, wanting to believe him but recalling that she'd believed Sean, too.

"Don't fight it, Addie..." he whispered as if he knew what was going through her mind.

And the truth was, she didn't want to fight it. He was offering her everything—raising Poppy as her mom, himself and a life with him.

And while it seemed too good to be true, he'd proven to her that she could trust him. That she could rely on him. So how could she deny herself any of what he was laying at her feet?

"You're sure..." she asked again, this whisper almost inaudible.

"Never more sure of anything in my life," he responded firmly. "I'm so in love with you I can hardly breathe when you walk out of the room."

"I love you, too," she finally said. "So much it scares me..."

He pulled her up against him, wrapped his arms tight enough around her to give her more of that strength she'd found in him. "I know the feeling," he confided as she rested her cheek to his chest. "But I think we can work it out."

"Married... Here, in Merritt..." she said.

"Married. Here, in Merritt. For the rest of the life we'll get to build together," he answered her awe with dedication.

For a moment Addie closed her eyes, melted into the monument that was the man, and let it all sink in.

He was hers…

Then, when she finally relaxed and genuinely accepted that, she opened her eyes again, reared back far enough to look up at him once more and teased him, "This place *does* need a lot of work…"

"We're back to the handyman thing?" he pretended offense.

"I do need a good one."

"I come at a high price."

"Yeah, over and over and over again last night…" she countered.

He grinned. "I love you, lady."

"I don't know how it happened, but I love you, too," she said, the gravity of it echoing in her voice.

His grin turned into a smile of gratitude, of relief. "So you *will* marry me?"

"I will. But it'll be a scandal."

The grin returned. "I think we can get through it. And you'll keep teaching me how to be a dad to your daughter?"

Those silly tears flooded her eyes again for no reason Addie could explain except that it meant so much to her that he'd set his own claims aside to give her heart's desire in Poppy. "I will."

For a moment their eyes held and then Tanner bent down to kiss her in a way that made her as much his as he was hers.

Which something inside Addie told her was how it would always be.

* * * * *

**WE HOPE YOU ENJOYED
THIS BOOK FROM**

Believe in love. Overcome obstacles. Find happiness.

Relate to finding comfort and strength in the
support of loved ones and enjoy the journey
no matter what life throws your way.

6 NEW BOOKS AVAILABLE EVERY MONTH!

HSEHALO2021

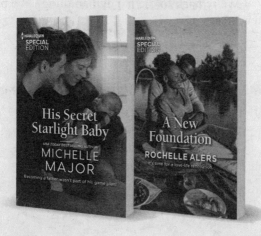

*Uplifting or passionate,
heartfelt or thrilling—
Harlequin has your
happily-ever-after.*

With a wide range of romance series that each
offer new books every month, you are sure to
find the satisfying escape you deserve.

Look for all Harlequin series
new releases on the
last Tuesday of each month
in stores and online!

Harlequin.com

HONSALE0521

COMING NEXT MONTH FROM
(H) HARLEQUIN
SPECIAL EDITION

YOU CAN FIND MORE INFORMATION ON UPCOMING HARLEQUIN TITLES, FREE EXCERPTS AND MORE AT HARLEQUIN.COM.

HSECNM0521

SPECIAL EXCERPT FROM

H HARLEQUIN

SPECIAL EDITION

*Since she first met him months ago in Rambling Rose
at the Hotel Fortune, Arabella Fortune has fantasized
about sexy and sweet Jay Cross. Now she sets to find ou*
how he'd intended to finish his last words to her:
"I think you should know…"

Read on for a sneak peek at
Cowboy in Disguise,
the final book in
The Fortunes of Texas: The Hotel Fortune
by New York Times *bestselling author Allison Leigh!*

"I think you'd better kiss me," she murmured, and he
cheeks turned rosy.

"Yeah?" His voice dropped also.

"If you don't, then I'll know this is just a dream."

"And if I do?"

She moistened her lips. "Then I'll know this is just a
dream."

He smiled slightly. He brushed the silky end of he
ponytail against her cheek and leaned closer. "Dream
Bella," he whispered, and slowly pressed his lips to hers

He felt her quick inhale and his own quick rush. Taste
the brightness of lemonade, the sweetness of strawberry

He slid his fingers from her ponytail to the back of her neck and urged her closer.

Her fingers splayed against his chest. She murmured something against his lips. He barely heard. His head was full of sound. Full of pulse beats and bells.

She murmured again. This time not against his lips.

He frowned, feeling entirely thwarted. "What?"

She pulled back yet another inch. Her fingertips pushed instead of urged closer. "Do you want to answer that?"

It made sense then. His cell phone was ringing.

Don't miss
Cowboy in Disguise *by Allison Leigh,*
available June 2021 wherever
Harlequin Special Edition books and ebooks are sold.

Harlequin.com

Copyright © 2021 by Harlequin Books S.A.

Get 4 FREE REWARDS!

We'll send you 2 FREE Books plus 2 FREE Mystery Gifts.

Harlequin Special Edition books relate to finding comfort and strength in the support of loved ones and enjoying the journey no matter what life throws your way.

FREE
Value Over
$20

YES! Please send me 2 FREE Harlequin Special Edition novels and my 2 FREE gifts (gifts are worth about $10 retail). After receiving them, if I don't wish to receive any more books, I can return the shipping statement marked "cancel." If I don't cancel, I will receive 6 brand-new novels every month and be billed just $4.99 per book in the U.S. or $5.74 per book in Canada. That's a savings of at least 12% off the cover price! It's quite a bargain! Shipping and handling is just 50¢ per book in the U.S. and $1.25 per book in Canada.* I understand that accepting the 2 free books and gifts places me under no obligation to buy anything. I can always return a shipment and cancel at any time. The free books and gifts are mine to keep no matter what I decide.

235/335 HDN GNMP

Name (please print)

Address   Apt. #

City   State/Province   Zip/Postal Code

Email: Please check this box ☐ if you would like to receive newsletters and promotional emails from Harlequin Enterprises ULC and its affiliates. You can unsubscribe anytime.

Mail to the **Harlequin Reader Service:**
IN U.S.A.: P.O. Box 1341, Buffalo, NY 14240-8531
IN CANADA: P.O. Box 603, Fort Erie, Ontario L2A 5X3

Want to try 2 free books from another series? Call 1-800-873-8635 or visit www.ReaderService.com.

*Terms and prices subject to change without notice. Prices do not include sales taxes, which will be charged (if applicable) based on your state or country of residence. Canadian residents will be charged applicable taxes. Offer not valid in Quebec. This offer is limited to one order per household. Books received may not be as shown. Not valid for current subscribers to Harlequin Special Edition books. All orders subject to approval. Credit or debit balances in a customer's account(s) may be offset by any other outstanding balance owed by or to the customer. Please allow 4 to 6 weeks for delivery. Offer available while quantities last.

Your Privacy—Your information is being collected by Harlequin Enterprises ULC, operating as Harlequin Reader Service. For complete summary of the information we collect, how we use this information and to whom it is disclosed, please visit our privacy notice located at corporate.harlequin.com/privacy-notice. From time to time we may also exchange your personal information with reputable third parties. If you wish to opt out of this sharing of your personal information, please visit readerservice.com/consumerschoice or call 1-800-873-8635. **Notice to California Residents**—Under California law, you have specific rights to control and access your data. For more information on these rights and how to exercise them, visit corporate.harlequin.com/california-privacy.

HSE21

From #1 *New York Times* bestselling author

LINDA LAEL MILLER

comes a brand-new Painted Pony Creek series.

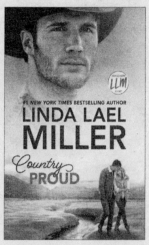

A story about three best friends whose strength, honor and independence exemplify the Montana land they love.

"Linda Lael Miller creates vibrant characters and stories I defy you to forget."
—#1 *New York Times* bestselling author Debbie Macomber

Order your copies today!

HQN

HQNBooks.com

PHLLBPA0521

Love Harlequin romance?

DISCOVER.

Be the first to find out about promotions,
news and exclusive content!

f Facebook.com/HarlequinBooks

Twitter.com/HarlequinBooks

Instagram.com/HarlequinBooks

Pinterest.com/HarlequinBooks

ReaderService.com

EXPLORE.

Sign up for the Harlequin e-newsletter and
download a free book from any series at
TryHarlequin.com

CONNECT.

Join our Harlequin community to
share your thoughts and connect
with other romance readers!
Facebook.com/groups/HarlequinConnection

HSOCIAL2(